THE LOCKER EXCHANGE

ANN RAE

the
LOCKER
EXCHANGE

a novel

wattpad books

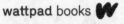

wattpad books

An imprint of Wattpad WEBTOON Book Group

Content Warning: death

Published in Canada by Wattpad WEBTOON Book Group, a division of Wattpad Corp.
36 Wellington Street E., Suite 200, Toronto, ON M5E 1C7 Canada

www.wattpad.com

First Wattpad Books edition: July 2022
ISBN 978-1-98936-583-0 (Trade Paper original)
ISBN 978-1-98936-584-7 (eBook edition)

Library and Archives Canada Cataloguing in Publication
information is available upon request.

Printed and bound in Canada

1 3 5 7 9 10 8 6 4 2

Cover design by Mumtaz Mustafa
Images © Hrytsiv Oleksandr via Shutterstock

THE LOCKER EXCHANGE

CHAPTER ONE

IT SHOULD HAVE BEEN DARKER.

My foot crunched a fallen brown leaf as I left the school and headed toward an empty student parking lot. It was close to eight at night, which meant my white Jeep sat alone, sun reflecting off it at low angles. There was something odd about having the light over my shoulder just before it began its descent into darkness.

The fall air bit at my heels and cheeks, prompting me to quicken my pace as I drew closer to the Jeep and tugged open the heavy door.

My backpack slid off my shoulder as I tossed it into the passenger seat and collapsed, exhausted from filing paperwork for different classes. I was an office aide at my high school, which meant I had a "responsibility" to assist. It was still only the second week of classes, and I'd been filing student schedules, requests for class changes, and the like for hours. I hadn't signed up for helping after school, though, and vowed then and there to never do it again.

I shook my head at the memory of all the forms I'd dealt with that day and reached forward to start the Jeep. All I wanted now was to listen to some music and enjoy a peaceful drive back home. Just as my fingers barely brushed against the volume dial, an ear-splitting screech shot through the air, and I recoiled in shock, my head shooting upward.

Anticipation took hold of my heart.

I waited in silence for it to come again. Maybe I'd imagined it, or, more realistically, I hoped I'd imagined it. I wasn't equipped for this kind of situation, and my eyes skimmed my car for anything I could use just in case I wasn't hallucinating.

"Help!"

The desperate, distant scream shook me into motion, and I bolted up, scrambling for the phone in my car's cupholder. I knew I should've called the police, but there had been a few incidents on the news that didn't necessarily showcase their abilities, so I dialed someone I trusted.

"Hello?" a deep voice answered. My heart was thumping so loudly I was sure he could hear it.

"Thank God." I almost gasped. "Baylor, I'm in the parking lot at school, and no one else is here, but I heard a scream and then someone yell for help, and I want to go check—"

"Stop," my older brother said sternly. Even from miles away at college, he could still command and I'd listen. "Call the police and get out of there. It's not safe."

"What if I call them and it's too late? I need to go over there now, at least to check, or I won't be able to sleep tonight. I thought I'd ask you to stay on the line with me. You know, just in case."

"Are you wearing a hoodie?" he asked finally. "Cover your face as much as you can."

Luckily, I had a spare one in the car.

My arms trembled as I hurriedly threw it on and leapt out of the Jeep. Adrenaline coursed through my blood like I'd never felt before. I'd learned about this before, the fight-or-flight response, but I never thought I'd experience it so vividly. I crept in the direction of the noise, my breathing hitched, unconsciously treading on the balls of my feet.

When I turned the corner, it was still. The football field looked empty, but my hands still quivered.

"Do you see anything?" Baylor asked quietly. His voice was calm. I couldn't necessarily say his virtual presence was soothing, but it was still better than being alone.

As my lips formed the shape of *no*, a sudden movement attracted my gaze. A black figure loomed at the top of the bleachers before noticing my position and flinching. Sudden panic propelled my body forward in a desperate attempt to get a better look, but the man ducked down behind the bleachers, scurrying past the fence and out of my sight.

"I just saw someone—" I started, determined to get another glance as I stepped forward.

Then all my courage vanished.

I felt it against my shoe. Something warm. Wet.

"Baylor," I whispered, my eyes shut tight as I willed my lips not to tremble.

"What? What happened?"

"I..."

I didn't want to look. I didn't know what it was, but the guesses swarming my mind were enough to make me hesitate. Yet I knew I had to, and, with a daring I didn't typically possess, my eyes slowly swept the bleachers, then the cement, and finally the puddle of blood mixed in a whirlpool of soaked blond hair.

MY JEEP WAS NO LONGER ALONE. Red and blue lights flashed against the now consuming dark as Colorado police strolled around the scene of Westwood High. I crossed my arms around my chest, relying on my own warmth as I shrank into a body that shook.

"Did you find him?" I asked again as a man in a uniform walked past. I stood up from where I'd been leaning on the hood of my car; while being surrounded by the authorities wasn't necessarily the most comfortable situation ever, I needed answers. "The guy who was on the stairs."

He didn't seem to hear me.

"Hello?"

His eyes almost rolled as he turned in my direction. "No."

"No, you didn't find him?" I asked for clarification.

"We didn't find him. And we probably won't, but we're doing a sweep of the area just in case you really did see someone."

"What?" I gawked at him. "What do you mean 'really did see someone'? You think I made it up?"

"Look," he said, shadows outlining his glum face. "We got your report and all your information. Thank you for cooperating, but you should head home. It's late, and there's nothing else you can do. We have it under control."

"Wait!" I started, but he was already tilting a hat over his eyes and turning away. "I'm not lying! Wait!"

I tried countless others, asking them the same questions about the victim and the murderer, but all I got were impassive looks and short replies. My blood boiled as I finally sank into my car and slammed the door shut.

"I DON'T GET IT," I fumed, my hand clutching a silver fork. My parents sat across from me, both chasing their pasta around in an uncomfortable silence. "They said their 'early investigation' indicates she tripped and fell, but I literally told them what I saw! Why don't they believe me?"

"Honey," my mom started, finally meeting my gaze. Her irises were a smoky gray with smile creases sharpening the edges of her eyes. I'd always been told I looked like her, as we shared the same color eyes and full lips, but it was only recently that I'd begun to see the resemblance. "I know tonight was rough, and I'm sorry you had to experience any of it, but we should be thankful they don't consider you a suspect. Right?"

She looked helplessly at my father, who had just raised a bite of spaghetti toward his mouth. He lowered it and let out an awkward cough. "Right. I mean, it's lucky they caught you on the surveillance cameras in the school and the parking lot. It could have gone a lot worse than it did. Thankfully you've always been lucky, Brynn."

Lucky? They thought the fact that I'd stumbled upon a murderer and watched as he got away was lucky?

"What aren't you guys understanding? Do you think I just made it up too?" I accused, anger biting at my words.

"No, that's not it," my mom said hastily. She set her fork down and sighed. "Your dad and I have something to tell you, and we would've told you earlier, but the decision was very last minute. It's just . . . well, the timing couldn't be worse."

"What?" I asked. This was why they'd waited until I got home to have dinner. A hole began to form in the pit of my stomach as I waited for them to tell me their news.

"Well," she started, her eyes drifting aimlessly before coming back to me, "we're going on a business trip. I'm not exactly sure how long it'll be, but we were told it could last at least a month, maybe more." Her expression pleaded with me. "I'm so sorry, honey. We didn't think something like this would happen, and we tried to reschedule, but it was too late."

My parents worked in programming. I knew they used to do freelance stuff until Baylor and I came along, but now they worked for a corporation in the city that focused on creating websites and gathering intel. Trips weren't uncommon in their line of business, but I still didn't like it. Why did they have to leave now of all times? It was like the fates were laughing at me. "Where are you guys going?"

"California," my dad said. The circles under his eyes had gotten darker lately, and both my parents had hair that was starting to gray. My hair was a similar shade of brown to theirs, muted, dark, so sometimes I wondered if I'd look like them as I approached their age.

It was hard watching as they got older, and having them so far away always made me feel uneasy. I'd never really been left alone for long periods of time, mostly because Baylor would stay with me if they went on vacation by themselves. As a junior in high school, I didn't get too many opportunities for independence, but right now, it wasn't something I wanted. I was close with my parents, and, although I didn't want to admit it, I felt vulnerable after what had just happened.

And now they were leaving.

"You really have to go?" I asked in a faint voice. I didn't want them to, but it felt like I didn't have a choice.

"Unfortunately," my dad said, grasping my hand from across the table. His skin felt soft, fragile, and I gripped it tight. "Baylor will come up from school on the weekends to keep you company. We know you've missed him since he started college, so hopefully you guys can use this time to catch up." His smile didn't reach his eyes, but I could appreciate the forced optimism.

The part about Baylor visiting wasn't so bad. He was three years older than me, a sophomore in college, and we'd always been close. Baylor was adopted, which made it funny when people would say he looked like either of our parents because, of course, he didn't. Everything about him contrasted with me: his tanned skin, sandy hair, and bright golden eyes. The sun and the clouds, that's how I always imagined the pair of us.

Not that I was gloomy or anything.

"When are you guys leaving?" I asked.

They shared that look again. A look of uneasiness, like they were delivering news about something dreadful.

"Tonight."

I launched out of my chair. "*Tonight?*"

"After dinner," my mom said. "But we'll be back soon, I promise. It'll be like we were never gone."

Somehow, that seemed doubtful.

Dinner didn't last very long after that, even though I tried to drag it out as much as I could by taking small bites and asking for more water about ten times. Finally, there was nothing left I could do.

They brought their suitcases downstairs and gave me hugs so tight I thought I would break. My mother's knuckles turned white as her fingers laced together, and, when I caught her glance, she gave one more guilt-laden smile. With wistful expressions on their faces, they waved good-bye, but just before leaving, my dad looked back.

"We love you. Call us anytime."

I gave him a nod despite wanting to fight for them to stay. I'd done enough fighting tonight. "Love you."

Our eyes locked for a long second before I shut the door behind them and watched from the window as the bright lights of their car faded into black.

Then I stood alone in a house too big for a girl too close to tears.

I DIDN'T GO TO SCHOOL THE NEXT DAY.

I felt like my trauma from seeing a dead body was a good enough excuse to lie on my bed and stare at the ceiling for hours on end. Luckily, Baylor saw my point and called the school to let them know I was suffering from a "cold."

My friends, however, were a bit more relentless.

"Are you sure you don't want to just stop by? Maybe it'll help get your mind off things," Adalia, one of my best friends, said through the speaker on my phone. She had a high voice, but it was the type that soothed you, the type that made you feel like someone was listening to your problems instead of judging.

"Yeah!" a deeper voice chimed. "We miss you!"

"Whatever, Liam." I scoffed, but I couldn't help the smile forming on my lips. "You guys saw me yesterday."

"So, it's been a whole day! That's enough time to, like, I don't know, move to another state. Wait, ow—" he yelped, and I figured Adalia had given him a punch. "I didn't mean her parents! I was just giving an example!"

"Well, think of a better one!" Adalia said.

"You guys are way too energetic for me right now. I'll come to school tomorrow, so don't worry too much," I said, shaking my head. I wasn't that upset at Liam's choice of words, but it reminded me once again why I was feeling so dull inside. It was nice having friends who listened, and I wanted to be in good shape when I saw them again. At least, better shape than I was right now.

"All right. Text us if you're bored!" Adalia replied. After agreeing to her terms, I ended the call and plopped right back onto my comforter.

Only a few seconds passed before the screen lit up again, and I rolled to my side, bringing my phone toward my face. I'd expected it to be a text from those two, but the email notification caught my attention, and I opened a message from the school.

Brynn Hastings (and parents),
This is a final notice for gym lockers. Today is the last day
to get assigned a locker number, so please stop by the office

before 4:00 p.m. If not, you will be unable to use the lockers during and outside of PE.

I groaned. *Of course.* Of course, something like this would happen. I'd been slacking a little, sure, but why did my timing have to be so bad?

I recalled my dad's words: *You've always been lucky, Brynn.* Yeah, right.

By the time I got to school, the hallways were empty. Those who had stayed back were out on the field or practicing in the gym for school sports. I looked ridiculous pairing one of Baylor's old hoodies with loose sweats, but I didn't care. I was mourning the loss of a free afternoon.

The infamous **MAIN OFFICE** sign felt menacing as it stared at me from above. I'd been in that office until late last night, and I was anything but happy to be back.

"Excuse me?" I peeked my head into the room, hoping that everyone hadn't run away at the first sound of the bell. There was a woman perched at the main desk, but she made no reply.

I walked toward her, but I still had to stand there for a while before she finally noticed me.

"Excuse me," I said again, tired of having to convince people to listen to me.

The lady looked up, tilted her glasses down, then gave a vicious scowl. Her hair was in short, uneven curls, and her eyes squinted in an unamused manner. The lipstick she wore was too heavy and had smeared, since it was the end of the day. It was obvious we both wanted to leave.

"What can I help you with?" she asked, uninterested.

I tried to keep my expression calm. I wanted to get this over with as soon as possible, and starting a fight didn't seem like the best way. "I got an email telling me to come in to get a locker number."

"What's your name?" Her eyes drooped.

"Brynn Hastings."

The woman didn't respond, but the typing coming from her keyboard gave me hope that she'd heard me.

I didn't know if she was always like this, but I was guessing it wasn't personal. I mean, I didn't know her. She wasn't the one I worked with during fifth period, and though she always sat at this desk, she never seemed to look up unless she was called.

Finally, the keyboard pecking came to a halt, and she tore off a sticky note, jotted down a number, then slapped it onto the counter in front of me. "This is the last locker in there, so no changes."

I had never known how in demand school gym lockers were.

"Thanks," I said as I took the note.

Silence.

I figured that was all I'd get, so I quickly scurried out of the office, glad our odd interaction was over.

Glassy brick walls curved into two separate entrances for the locker room: one for the girls and one for the boys. It was a little different from the typical high school model. The only thing that separated the boys and girls was a wall of lockers, which basically meant we all shared a giant room split in the middle. Luckily, there was a thin, solid wall that rose from above where the boys' and girls' lockers divided the room all the way to the ceiling, which drowned out the noise from the guys' side of the room.

I had gym during my third period, but I always blocked out the memory. The only thing that made it bearable was Adalia's presence, though even I had to admit she was more athletic than I was. I liked dancing, but if there was a ball involved? Count me out.

The only reason I was even taking gym was because I could only use outside sources, like my past dance classes, for two years. Unfortunately, I needed three years of physical education in order to graduate, so here I was.

I glanced at the piece of paper and sighed.

Of course, I got a locker right in the middle of the dividing wall. At least I got the top half, which was about two feet wide and stopped just above my eye level.

I spun the lock to the numbers written on the note and pulled the handle toward me. The door came to a jolting halt, then rested on its hinges as I peered in.

Then I paused.

Was that a poster on the back of the wall? I reached my hand out, just a little, to see if it touched the back. But there was no back, just air. And abs.

I swear there were abs.

"Like what you see?" a deep voice asked from the other side of the locker. My feet stumbled backward before I caught myself and realized what was going on. With widened eyes, I bent forward to get a clearer view.

There was no back wall to my locker. It connected directly to the locker that opened on the boys' side.

And here was a boy.

"What?" I sputtered. I'd never been in this kind of situation before. Sure, I'd seen shirtless guys; I had an older brother. But this definitely wasn't my older brother. "Where's your shirt? Shouldn't there be a back to this locker?"

The voice answered, neglecting the first question. "There should be," he started to say, his body tilting down so I could see better. His face was tan, narrow, complemented with dark eyebrows that arched in amusement as his gaze locked with mine.

I recognized those eyes: the blue of the winter sky, glassy in its reflection through icicles, seemed trapped in the eyes of a boy with a conceited grin. "But there isn't."

I knew who he was. Almost everyone at Westwood did.

That was Kyler Fellan.

CHAPTER TWO

"SO, YOU SHARE A LOCKER WITH A REALLY HOT GUY."
Adalia elbowed my side as we made our way into the first class
of the new day. A few other classmates shuffled into the room,
some pulling off hoodies, others making fun of them, since this
was Colorado and we would just get cold again later.

Adalia wasn't wearing a hoodie, though. My best friend
liked to experiment with her look, and today's was one of my
favorites. She wore a tucked-in sweater and wide-legged jeans
with her hair half-up. She was a shorter girl with long blond
hair, dark emerald eyes, and a smile that was sweet enough
to trust. That trust meant she knew everything happening at
Westwood, including the rumors about Kyler.

I still couldn't believe I'd opened my gym locker yesterday to
find the one and only—and half-naked—Kyler staring back at
me with an unashamed grin. Adalia and Liam had been making
fun of me nonstop since I'd told them on the phone, and it only
seemed to emphasize that this year was off to an unnatural start.

"It could be worse," she said.

I rolled my eyes playfully at Adalia before shrugging my

backpack off. "When you put it like that, sure. But it's Kyler. I don't know if I really want to get close to him."

"Kyler Fellan, the type to never get serious," Adalia stated, taking the seat next to me. "He's charming, smart, reserved, and superhot. Only Sterling Reyes comes close. They're best friends, but they're complete—"

"Opposites. Yes, yes, like I haven't heard you give this speech a hundred times before." I smiled at her to let her know I was kidding, but I felt the corners of my lips sink. "Besides, I'm worried about other things right now."

Adalia shifted uncomfortably. "Me too. I can't believe they didn't find the guy who pushed her."

"I know. It doesn't seem like they're looking too hard," I said from the edge of my seat.

"But he's a murderer," Adalia said.

Exasperation flooded my expression as I fell back farther into my chair. "That's what I said. It's like they don't even care." Suddenly I leaned forward, letting my eyes skim the room before whispering in her direction, "What if he's a high school student?"

"Then he could be anywhere," she murmured. With a shudder, her green eyes found the floor. "It's pretty scary."

The two of us sat in silence, thoughts of terror and fear hanging over us. The rest of the school seemed to be feeling the same way; usually the classroom was full of sleepy laughter, but that had turned into low-level mumbles.

Adalia placed a hand on my knee as a gesture of reassurance, but the solemn expression remained etched on my face. "I'm sure the school will make an announcement later so students will be careful." Adalia paused and put a finger on her chin. "Well, at least around stairs."

At that last comment, my head snapped up. I couldn't help the amused smile sneaking onto my lips. "That's a bad joke."

"Who said I'm joking?" She laughed, her platinum hair bouncing along to the airy pitch.

The chiming sound was cut off as our teacher entered the room. Taking her position at the front of the room, she snapped at the class, "Quiet, please."

Adalia gave me another look before facing forward. Others raced to do the same before Mrs. Drella decided to turn around again.

With a spin of her heels, she faced the classroom with an expression that seemed softer than her usual hardened look. There was a long pause before her lips finally parted. "As your first-period teacher, I'm obligated to let you know some unfortunate news."

Adalia and I traded looks. So did others in the room.

"Two nights ago, a student many of you know. . ." She stopped, as if trying to figure out the best phrasing. "Erm, Ingrid. Ingrid Lund, a junior, suffered from a fatal accident near the football field. Truly, truly terrible." She sighed. "It's unfortunate that I have to deliver news like this. Please be careful so accidents like this don't repeat—"

My hand shot up.

"Miss Hastings?"

"I was there that night," I said, trying to keep the anger out of my words. The room went silent as I continued. "I saw someone at the top of the stairs, and I don't think she tripped. The school should be warning us to watch out at night, or they should at least add some extra security."

Mrs. Drella's lips pursed. "If you have more information or evidence, see me after class. Otherwise, I think that's enough. There's no need to scare your fellow students."

"They should be scared," I muttered. My teeth began to grind as our teacher cleared her throat and reached for a stack of papers behind her.

"Let's start class."

Mrs. Drella stopped at each row of desks, passing out papers that probably wouldn't get done until tomorrow morning, and when a certain black-haired boy turned around to hand me my own, my heartbeat did a leap.

A very small leap.

Sterling Reyes. He'd been sitting in front of me every day since school began. Every day, he gave me one of those loose smiles and then faced forward, ready to start the day fresh, as if we weren't all dying from the horrors of public school and, more realistically, murderers.

I'd admit he made my heart flutter sometimes. And now that I was able to see his face, a sense of calm washed over me, my previous biting anger subsiding just a bit when he smiled. The sight of his dimpled cheeks and warm umber eyes always had that effect on me, but I'd never really done much about it.

"Morning," he said in a low voice before turning his focus away from me. It was so casual that I didn't think he expected a reply, so I smiled back instead.

Sterling had something most guys didn't.

He had manners. He was polite. He cared about other people.

Simply put, he was a nice person. Boys like that were hard to find in general, and especially in our school. So with a face and personality like Sterling's, it was almost impossible not to feel a little attracted to him.

Unfortunately, I couldn't stare at his back all day and squinted past him instead. Mrs. Drella started hitting her marker against the smart board, writing letters and words that I never paid attention to because learning history was fun and all, but add a monotone voice and constant lectures? Not really my thing.

My thoughts began to drift, and a feeling of smallness settled in my chest again. It was obvious I needed to do something, not just for everyone at school but for Ingrid too. I knew she'd been involved in something bigger than an "accident," and I wasn't going to just let it go.

However, it was daunting. Realistically speaking, what could someone like me do? I was just a junior in high school who didn't even have her parents at home to help her.

But now Ingrid's parents didn't have a daughter.

What if another student found themselves alone, unsuspecting, and that murderer came back for round two? What if the next victim was someone I knew? A friend?

My stomach knotted at the thought.

I hadn't known Ingrid that well, but I knew no one deserved to be written off like that.

She'd called for help, and I'd failed her.

I wasn't going to fail again.

—

I MARCHED INTO SECOND PERIOD with newfound determination. My brows furrowed as I fell into my seat and pulled out my notebook, my pen tapping the page as I thought of a plan. I needed to do something about Ingrid, but I didn't know anything about her. I couldn't just find the guy who'd pushed her, either, not that I particularly wanted to.

Maybe I could convince the school to at least issue some warnings. Even if she hadn't been murdered, which she had, safety was always important when it came to teenagers, right?

My head drooped to the side as I began writing the plan down but shot up again when a familiar face walked by my desk.

Kyler glanced down and smiled. "Hey, locker buddy."

He continued down the aisle silently and slid into the seat behind me. I'd been so focused on Ingrid that I hadn't even thought about the awkwardness of sitting right in front of him after yesterday's encounter.

We'd never talked before that. We'd never had a reason to, but I guessed sharing a locker counted as one now.

He was popular, and I knew bits and pieces about him because Adalia liked to keep track of those kinds of details. One reason for his fame was obvious, though. He had the kind of face that girls liked.

His nose was straight, symmetrical, and he had sharp eyes that flared upward with dark eyelashes to top them off. It didn't help that his gaze was so penetrating; he could see everything you didn't want him to.

I didn't trust pretty boys like him.

He probably didn't trust a lot of people, either, especially not after his family tragedy became the subject of gossip around school. Kyler's dad had died in a car accident last year; unfortunately, everyone knew about it. I guessed it came with the territory when you were as popular as he was. I felt bad that I knew. I wasn't close to him, and something like that wasn't a stranger's business.

Adalia and Liam made up my friend group, and I wasn't trying to climb our school hierarchy by interacting with Kyler. I liked where I was. People knew of me, I knew of them, and if we talked it wasn't uncomfortable. I had some classroom friends that I liked, but all my time and energy went toward the two I cherished the most.

Kyler, on the other hand, was known by everyone.

I couldn't imagine how exhausting that would be. He seemed unbothered by it, though, with an unfalteringly cool expression, as if nothing could get to him. Everything was amusing. Nothing was serious.

I pulled my thoughts away from him as class began with a teacher who was much nicer than Mrs. Drella, and I tried to forget about the overwhelming presence coming from behind me. For the majority of class, I'd done a pretty good job of it . . . until we had to pass back pamphlets.

Kyler didn't seem to notice when I turned around.

His dusky hair was disheveled; it fell to the side, looking like a guided mess as his fingers ran through it. Then he glanced up, and my gaze shot away as if I were guilty of something.

I didn't realize how closely I'd been looking at him and cursed my curiosity then and there. His gaze shifted toward my hand and then the papers, and when he reached out to take them, his finger brushed against mine.

"Thanks," he said. His eyes were unwavering as the corners of his lips turned up, and I copied his smile.

"Yeah."

"LIAM, THAT'S DISGUSTING!" Adalia squealed as Liam moved closer to her with a picture of God-knows-what popped up on his phone screen. No one seemed to notice their performance despite the fact that we were in the middle of the cafeteria. Luckily, we usually got to sit alone during lunch. "Let me eat without feeling repulsed for once!"

Liam threw his head back, laughing as the two of us shook our heads in disapproval. Liam had dark hair that he'd always kept short and tawny brown skin. He was the definition of a typical teenage boy, and one day, we hoped he'd come to the realization that he was, in fact, an idiot.

That last part was a joke.

In reality, Liam was witty and caring, and despite the teasing the three of us dished out to each other, Liam would always be one of my best friends.

"C'mon, B. Tell her it's funny."

"It's not funny," I deadpanned.

"It's hilarious!" he replied, faking hurt as he pressed a hand against his heart. Immediately, his feigned shock turned into a widespread grin as he leaned across the table. "Wanna see?"

"No!" Adalia and I shouted in unison, but that only encouraged his laughter more. Adalia slapped her palm over his mouth, and having been around them for an extended amount of time, I knew what was coming next.

"Eww! You can't just lick people, Liam!" Adalia jumped out of her seat with a cry, maneuvering herself so that she was behind him. She caught him in a headlock that he hardly tried to escape. "Why are you like this?"

I rolled my eyes from across the table. "Why are either of you like this?"

I asked that, but I knew they were doing their best to distract me from getting caught up in my thoughts about Ingrid. I'd been thinking about what had happened all morning, and it was starting to take its toll on my mood. To be fair, though, most of the school was thinking about it too. I'd heard people talking about her in every class, every passing period, even when I'd gone to the bathroom.

I didn't know if that was a good thing or not.

My two friends simultaneously looked at me with eyes that complemented each other. With the same type of smile, they exchanged a look and then shrugged. "But you love us," Adalia piped.

"It's a wonder," I replied, shaking my head lightly, but Liam had already begun talking.

"Let's hang out tonight," he suggested, glancing toward me and then up at Adalia, who still had a firm hold on him. They were always touchy like that, and I knew Liam liked it more than he let on. It was obvious to everyone except Adalia. "It's been a while, and I know no one's at your house, Brynn. Unless you're secretly hiding some mysterious guy we don't know about . . ."

When I sighed instead of answering, Adalia's voice took on a higher pitch. "Maybe she is!"

"Who is it?" Liam stretched across the table eagerly, taking a very excited Adalia with him. "Do we know him?"

"You should," I said with a curt nod, "since he is a figment of your imagination."

"Smartass," mumbled Adalia, but she took back her seat next to Liam and grinned. "I wanna sleep over tonight."

"I will too," Liam added. But when he pulled out his phone, he scrunched his eyebrows together and let out a small groan. "Football practice gets out late tonight."

"What a jock," I joked, and he stuck out his tongue in response.

When he tucked his phone back into his pocket, he continued, "I've gone to almost every practice, unlike some people."

"Who are you talking about?" I asked. Adalia turned to face him with a curious expression as well.

"Your locker boyfriend." Liam smirked. "You know, Kyler. He almost never shows up to practice, and when he does, he's always late and his hair's a mess." He raised an eyebrow. "We can all guess why his hair's a mess."

"Aren't you just upset you're not getting as many girls as him, Liam?" Adalia joked with a ruffle of his hair. "That's why you started playing football in the first place, isn't it?"

"Of course not. I've already got two girls who can't keep their hands off me," he said with a wink at the two of us. When we laughed, Liam added, "I'll come over late."

He paused before continuing.

"I'll bring food."

—

"The death of a high schooler at Westwood, Ingrid Lund, is still under investigation. We're expecting to know the verdict soon, but as of now, signs seem to point toward an unfortunate accident. Joining us here today are her parents—"

"Should we watch something else?" Liam asked. His hand was frozen above the last burger left on the pile of takeout bags on the coffee table in front of us. The three of us were gathered around my living room TV after a late dinner.

I sat forward on the couch. "No. I want to see," I said. My grip was tight around the remote as I increased the volume on our local evening news. Two people, an older woman and a man with barely graying hair, were being interviewed. They looked about my parents' ages.

"We—I don't, I mean—I didn't know that something like this would . . ." The man took a deep breath after trampling over his words. "I'm sorry, I can't do this." His pale face was shell-shocked, and his sunken eyes looked like a rabbit's: antsy, paranoid, terrified.

His wife glanced at him with an unreadable expression, but the camera was no longer focused on them. Adalia squirmed in her chair as the next picture became clear, and I felt my stomach drop.

A deep red puddle sank into the cement right at the base of the bleacher steps. Luckily, the photos weren't too graphic, but I could still make out threads of pale hair weaving from the edges of the screen. A picture of her body under a sheet also came up, and only I knew how her arms and legs were bent at odd angles underneath the drape.

"Is that what you saw when you found her?" Adalia whispered as she shielded her eyes with her hands. "Are they allowed to show that?"

I tore my gaze away and tried to focus on Adalia instead. "Yeah. My . . . my foot hit her . . . head." The last word came out choked.

An uneasy sensation rose from the pit of my chest, and I curled over my legs, trying to stabilize myself. The sound of the TV shutting off prompted my head to tilt, and I felt Liam's calming hand on my back. "Hey, we don't have to talk about it. Not unless you want to."

Adalia gave an enthusiastic nod and hopped up from the recliner she'd been sitting in to cuddle up against my side. I gave them both a small smile.

Having them here made me feel more at ease, but I wasn't sure I wanted to talk it out with them—or with anyone. There were a lot of things I wanted to say, like how I felt disgusted with myself for being grossed out at the remains of someone who'd once been talking, laughing, breathing. Worse than that, I felt ashamed of myself. Maybe if I had put my hoodie on a little faster or ran when I first heard the scream, Ingrid would still be alive.

I deserved every nightmare I had about what I'd seen. I felt like such a bad person, and my friends were the last people I wanted to expose this side of myself to.

Finally, I shook my head. "Thanks, guys. It's okay. My parents are making me go to the school psychiatrist tomorrow, so I can talk about it then."

Adalia nodded. "Okay. But we'll always be here for you. Right, Liam?"

"Totally. We've been stuck together since third grade, so it's not just going to change now."

He was right. In third grade, the three of us had become attached at the hip when we were the only members of the Sandwich Club. It had seemed cool then, and we liked to throw pieces of bread at the ducks that floated on the pond near our school. We had meetings on the playground and would snack on PB&Js together.

"I remember when you caught a bug for Adalia and thought it was the best present ever," I added, a fond smile spreading on my lips. "She screamed."

Liam laughed. "That was a harsh rejection."

"That's not how you confess your feelings to a girl," she said, leaning forward and sending Liam a pointed look. "You should've gotten me Silly Bandz or something."

Liam raised his eyebrows. "And you would have said yes to my declaration of love?"

Adalia grinned. "No. Unfortunately for you, my one true love is Brynn." She let a shy laugh escape her lips and winked in my direction.

"I feel the same way, Ad." I shuffled into a new position on the couch. "We're ditching Liam."

"Hey, now, wait a minute," he interjected, making the three of us burst into laughter. When the noise died down after a while and the only sound left in the room was the faint noise of the pipes in the ceiling, Adalia spoke again.

"Thanks for being my friends, you guys. I don't know what I would do without you." Her head fell gently against my shoulder, and her light lashes fluttered closed. "And with that being said . . ." She smiled, her breathing soft and slow. "I think it's time to sleep."

CHAPTER THREE

MY NAILS PICKED AT EACH OTHER NERVOUSLY as I sat upright in a stiff, barely cushioned chair. The desk in front of me was empty except for scattered papers, a half-full mug of coffee, and a nameplate that read *Denise Jackson*.

The clock told me I'd arrived at the right time, but it wasn't very reassuring that my new psychiatrist was nowhere to be found. Anxiety began to pile on my shoulders as I waited for her, or, more specifically, waited to spill my deepest, darkest thoughts to a complete stranger. It wasn't like I really wanted to talk to anyone about my problems, but I understood that maybe bottling everything up wasn't a healthy coping mechanism.

Still, this was uncomfortable.

A windowed door swung open behind me just as I was about to get up and ask the neighboring office about her absence. Heels clacked against the hard floor as a woman with a messy bun locked eyes with me and gave an overbearing grin.

"Sorry about that," she said, clutching her purse in one hand and a salad in the other. Denise shook the salad container. "There was a line."

"Oh, um, that's all right."

She dropped her purse onto the desk with a clang as she threw herself into the seat and pulled out a laptop. Her typing was slow. "All right, let's see, let's see . . ." she said through chomps of gum. "Brynn, yeah?"

"Yes." I nodded.

"You don't have to be so stiff, girl!" Denise laughed, as if trying to ease the tension. It didn't work. "All right, so your parents wanted you to come in and see me because you were a witness to the accident that happened recently. Is that all correct?"

"Yeah."

"So you witnessed the incident? What was that like?" She cracked open the salad lid and began layering a rosy-colored dressing over the contents of the bowl.

"Um, well . . ." I tried to resist biting my nails. "It wasn't great."

Denise nodded enthusiastically before grappling the container with two hands and shaking vigorously. "And how are you feeling about everything?"

Another bubble smacked her lips.

My attempt to ignore all the distractions in front of me was futile. It was obvious she didn't care about what I was saying or how I felt and instead was running through routine questions like "How did that make you feel?" and "Do you want to talk about it?" which I no longer felt like doing. My eyebrows creased as I looked in her direction.

"The school isn't really helping."

"Hmm?" she hummed with unfocused eyes. She brought a tissue up to her mouth, and I could tell she was spitting out her gum now. "Why's that?"

I didn't care about being polite anymore. "The announce-ments were stupid. They just warned us to be careful so we don't 'fall' too."

Denise dug her fork into the salad. "Well, what else should they be saying?" she asked in between bites.

My eyes widened in disbelief. Was she serious? "They should be telling us to watch out for potential murderers, maybe?" I couldn't help the attitude that infused my words.

A cackle escaped her lips, but my expression soon turned that laugh into a pathetic excuse for a cough.

"Ahem," she said, her eyes darting as she cleared her throat. "Look, kids can act crazy, you know? The school just doesn't want to get everyone riled up for no reason."

"It's not for no reason," I muttered, finally having had enough and standing up. "You're obviously hungry, so I'm leaving."

This got Denise's attention. Her head snapped up quickly, midbite, and she tried to swallow it quickly. "What? What's wrong?"

"You are!" I spat, my hands flying in the air. "Everyone work-ing for the school is wrong here! No one's taking this seriously, and I don't get it. If this were anywhere else, the issue would have been handled differently. I wouldn't have to do anything." My gaze hardened one final time as I shot her a stone-cold glare. "Enjoy your salad."

Then I gripped the door handle tight and slammed it behind me with a frustration I knew might have been out of propor-tion. My hand ran through my hair; straight, dark strands fell back messily as I took a breath and tried to settle myself.

"Didn't go so well?" a familiar voice asked. It was smooth

and low, striking an unwilling chord in my chest as I looked in his direction. One of his long legs propped him up against the wall, and Kyler gave a wry smile, as if he'd witnessed something amusing.

Well, he probably had.

"Did you hear all that?" I asked, bringing my hand up to a warm cheek. I wasn't the type to blow my fuse easily, and a minute feeling of guilt was already starting to form.

"Only the last part," he said, straightening up. He wore a navy-blue hoodie that seemed to broaden his shoulders and brighten his eyes. "I was waiting to hand this in." Kyler held a form up with two long fingers and shrugged. "But the office seems busy."

I sent a look toward the **MAIN OFFICE** sign and tried to push down the unsettling feeling that now came with it. "They're always busy," I groused. "They made me stay here till eight a few nights ago."

I felt my expression darken at the memory as I turned the other way, but Kyler was quiet. I didn't know how much he knew about the situation with Ingrid or the fact that I had been involved, or if he'd even listened to the announcements at all.

I was tired of thinking about it. I'd noticed bags under my eyes that morning, but even concealer wasn't helping.

"She sucks, you know," Kyler finally said. "The only reason I went last year was because I got to skip out on math."

I hoped my face didn't reflect my surprise: I'd almost forgotten about what had happened to his dad. I didn't know how he felt about the fact that everyone knew. If I were him, I would've been bitter about it, never mentioning it if I didn't have to or calling out those who'd spread the rumors.

So I was taken aback when he spoke about it so casually, especially to me.

I tried to change the subject.

"I don't think I'm gonna go anymore." I tossed a look toward the door behind me before stepping away.

"Yeah?" Kyler chuckled. "What class are you missing?"

"Science." I found myself next to him as we walked into the hallway and turned toward another one lined with classroom doors and windows. "I think I'd rather learn about the power-house of the cell than watch her shake another salad."

Kyler looked at me, his gaze intense under long lashes. They brushed against his cheek when he blinked, and I had to tear my eyes away. "You know," he said, his words smooth and thought-ful in a way I'd never heard him speak before, "I never thought you'd be the type to blow up at school staff like that."

"Is that an insult?"

"No."

"I'm usually not." I decided to be honest. "I'm just so frus-trated lately. I don't think I've ever felt this upset before, and I guess it's starting to get to me."

"It's not a bad look," he said with a glint in his eye, and I had to suppress a laugh.

"What, are aggressive girls your type?" I raised an eyebrow at him, and this time, his laugh was a low chime.

"They could be."

"Well, I'm flattered," I started, "but not interested."

"Really?" His lips curved into a flirtatious grin. "Not at all?"

For some reason, I almost felt relieved. This was the Kyler

I'd heard about: he was cocky, playful, and never serious. The fact that he'd caught me at a vulnerable moment was just bad timing.

"I've got bigger things to worry about than boys."

I gave him a pointed look, but his laugh seemed laced with nothing but amusement.

"I'm serious," I said, crossing my arms.

Kyler's laugh slid into a smile—a smile that seemed daring, challenging even—and his eyes locked with mine.

"I know."

It was now Friday, and after a very long week, I was not in the mood for gym class. Of course, the locker room came with a new type of feeling now that I knew there was a boy sharing my locker—and not just any boy, but Kyler Fellan of all people. I was still trying to get used to it, and our conversation yesterday hadn't helped.

Luckily, I had a weekend ahead of me, and I didn't need to worry about seeing him at all.

As I grabbed a shirt from my locker, a familiar name piqued my interest, and I glanced that way, seeing two girls just a few feet away. One of them was standing at her locker, doing pretty much the same thing as me. The other was sitting on the bench, her finger brushing against the phone screen as she scrolled. "I don't really watch the news," she started, "but my parents do."

"Yeah?" the other girl said, her head inside her shirt. "And they were talking about Ingrid?"

"Yeah," the bench girl replied. "You know, my parents work

with hers, so we've had dinners together before. Just casual, you know? I mean, we hung out sometimes, but . . . her dad looked really bad on the TV. I could barely recognize him."

"Really?" The first girl peeked her head out. "He looked that different?"

Her friend nodded. "He's way skinnier than before, and kind of pale. My parents don't even talk to him anymore. They said he's kind of gone off the deep end."

"Wow, seriously? But he did just lose his daughter. He's probably having a hard time dealing."

Bench girl shook her head. "No, no. I mean before that."

Now I was intrigued. I'd seen the news, obviously, but I didn't know what he'd looked like before that. Was he really so different? What had happened in her family?

Once I was finished changing, I opened the door, threw my regular clothes back in, and slammed the locker door shut. It was so frustrating not having answers, but at least the gossip would keep me in the loop. Everyone always had something to say.

It was finally the weekend.

A golden-haired boy plopped onto the couch next to me and handed me a wrapped sandwich from a place he'd stopped by on his way down from school. "It's good," Baylor said, waving his own in front of my face. "This place is a local gem."

"Oh, you're an expert now?" I positioned my laptop on the coffee table in front of us and turned the camera on. The two of us didn't look great from the low angle, and I decided to prop it onto the flattest pillow I could find instead.

"I am, actually." He gave a proud smile. "You know, they recruited me to do campus tours because they thought my face was 'memorable.' That and I'm somewhat charming, if I do say so myself." He gave an over-the-top wink, and I let out a snort. "Anyway, I accepted. So now I know all the best spots on campus to eat and nap."

"And study?"

"I guess some of that too." Baylor glanced at the laptop screen and began unwrapping his sandwich. His hands were just as tan as his face, and the glow of his golden skin reflected just how often he spent time outside. "What time are they supposed to call us?"

"Any minute. They said one o'clock our time, and California is an hour behind us, right?"

"Yeah, it—"

Ring. Ring. Ring.

I almost jumped out of my skin at the high-pitched trills and quickly tapped Accept This Call. I knew there was no reason to feel nervous about talking to them, especially because they were my parents, but I always got a little shy when it came to calling people. It didn't help that I was so used to talking to my parents either in person or through text when they were home.

The excited faces of my parents popped up, their smiles grainy due to the camera quality and the lights that shone from behind them. "Hey!" My mom beamed, leaning forward in her seat. They seemed to be in a conference room, though it was empty from what I could see.

"Hey, Mom," Baylor said.

I gave a timid smile. "Hi."

"What are you guys up to over there?" my dad asked, placing his arm around my mother's shoulders. "Has anything exciting happened in the few days that we've been gone?"

My mind raced through the Rolodex of memories I'd gained since last seeing them. Lots were filled with Ingrid, but I wasn't too keen on talking about her, so I decided to land on something else. "Oh," I said. "Actually, something weird happened after you guys left."

My mom's thin eyebrows creased in worry. "Good or bad?"

"Neither, really." I tucked a strand of hair behind my ears. "Well, I was kind of late on getting a locker for gym class, so they gave me the last one. And it doesn't have a back to it."

Baylor almost choked on his sandwich, and the three of us threw him alarmed looks as he hit his chest and began coughing. Then his eyes settled on me. "Is it on the wall? Like, in the dividing wall in the middle?"

I'd forgotten that Baylor knew about the locker room design. His eyes, sharp and narrow, pleaded with me to say no, but I averted my gaze uncomfortably.

"It might be."

"Oh my God," Baylor exclaimed, setting his sandwich down. Then he turned toward our parents. "That means she shares a locker with some guy!"

They shared an unreadable look before the corners of my mother's lips twitched up, and she gave a quiet chuckle. "And it's the last one? You can't exchange it?"

I shook my head. "No, I don't think I can."

Baylor suddenly looped his arm over my shoulders and tapped

our foreheads together. His eyes bored into mine intensely, and I tried hard not to sigh. He was always protective when it came to boys, not that there was a real reason to be, considering I'd never even had a boyfriend before. "Always change with the door closed, okay? Or even better, change in the bathroom! Don't even talk to him."

"I wasn't going to take my clothes off in front of some guy!" I withdrew from his grip crossly and gestured toward the camera with a frown. "Are you guys hearing this?"

My dad's arms were crossed as he nodded. "Your brother's right."

"What?" Now my face was beginning to burn. "I'm not going to strip in front of him! Who do you think I am?"

My mother burst out in laughter, her eyes creasing as the airy sound resonated from our speakers. "Brynn, honey, they're just talking nonsense. I know you were never going to do anything like that in the first place." Then she gave an impish grin. "But . . . what's he like? Is he cute? Nice?"

"I . . ." My hands inched toward warm cheeks, and I tried to cool them down. "I mean . . ."

"She's smiling!" Baylor announced, appalled.

"He's cute, but it doesn't matter. I'm busy with other stuff, you know?"

My brother gave a firm nod. "Exactly, and—hey! Don't roll your eyes at me."

"I think she has the right to," my mom chimed in, winking at me. "Well, I'm glad you're having some fun at school, Brynn. Has anything else been going on?"

"Actually . . ." My voice came out quietly. "I don't think

it's going to work out with the school psychiatrist. We didn't exactly see eye to eye." .

"Oh," my dad said. He gave an encouraging smile and placed his hand over Mom's. "That's all right. You gave it a shot. Your mom and I will look for someone better for you to talk to, okay?"

"Okay." I was tired of talking about myself now and decided to drill them instead.

"How is work going?" I finally asked.

"It's going," Dad replied. His expression seemed tired now, as if the high of seeing his kids again was beginning to fade. The purple underlining his eyes was more defined than my mother's.

Unfortunately, he didn't get the power of makeup.

"We'd rather be home," she said. "Working all the time is never fun, even if we have a view of palm trees and beaches."

"Nothing beats the Rocky Mountains." My brother threw a glance toward our own window and grinned. "Are you guys jealous?"

"Ha! Yeah, right. Are *you* guys jealous?" my dad retorted, and I shook my head. They were so immature sometimes, but at least they were always there to lighten the mood.

"I prefer warm weather, you know," I said.

"Me too," my mom agreed. "We can come here together next time and leave the boys at home."

"Okay." I tried to give her the biggest smile I could muster before seeing my parents glance up at something behind their computer screen. My mom gave a dejected sigh.

"Unfortunately, it's time for us to get back to work." She gave us wistful looks through the screen. "Call us right away if anything happens, though. We might be in a different state, but we're still with you, okay?" She gave me a pointed look.

I gave a slow nod, and Baylor smiled. "Totally," he said. "Text us when you're free again."

"Of course," she replied. Our parents both waved. "Talk soon!"

The call ended, and the screen was suddenly dark with their absence.

"Guess you can finally eat your sandwich now," Baylor said. "Do you want me to heat it up?"

"Oh." I'd completely forgotten about it. "Sure."

He brought it to the kitchen and began shouting over the microwave. "Wanna play games? I bought some new ones for the Switch."

I threw him a thumbs-up and smiled.

It was hard to get lost in my depressing thoughts when Baylor was there, constantly taking care of me or getting my mind off things that would otherwise dampen my mood.

Luckily, his games helped with that too.

CHAPTER FOUR

THE WEEKEND WENT BY QUICKLY. Baylor and I had played games until three o'clock in the morning on Saturday, which was fun despite the fact that I lost almost every round. On Sunday, Adalia and Liam came over for a movie night, and Baylor made his special hot chocolate, which was just normal hot chocolate with freeze-dried marshmallows in it.

The lively weekend only made this class-plagued Monday feel long and dull. By the end of seventh period, I couldn't stop my leg from bouncing in anticipation of the bell, and when it finally came, I almost stumbled out of my chair from rushing.

Finally.

I popped in my earbuds and scrolled through old playlists, searching for a song that fit the mood. I wanted something cheerful, something to lift my mood after a day of taking tests and enduring lectures for hours on end. When I finally found the right song, I sank my phone into my pocket and headed for my Jeep. Adalia was supposed to meet me in the parking lot since I'd taken her to school due to her own car troubles.

I was surprised to see that my Jeep was empty when I finally arrived. I'd taken my time, trying to savor the effects of carefree music, so it was odd that she hadn't gotten here before me.

Just as I slid into the car, my music was interrupted by a different song—Adalia's ringtone, to be specific. A picture of her face being shoved into an ice cream cone suddenly lit up my screen, and I tapped my finger against the green Accept button.

"Hey," I said, turning on the speaker as I shrugged off my backpack. "Where are you?"

"You didn't read the group messages, did you?" Her high-pitched voice turned into a sigh.

"Group messages?" My eyebrows furrowed in confusion before I realized why I hadn't gotten any. "Oh sorry. I had a test today, so I turned my phone on Do Not Disturb. Why? What's up?"

"Do you want to watch Liam's football practice? Since we're hanging out after school, we thought it might be easier to just wait for him and then get food together afterward. If you want to go home and meet him later, we can totally do that too."

"Yeah, sure. Meeting up now sounds fine. Where are you?"

"I'm on the bleachers."

"Okay, cool, I'll meet you there. Save me a seat?" I asked, leaning behind my seat and digging for a jacket I'd thrown somewhere in the back.

"Already done! See you!"

The line went dead, and my original music continued. I threw on a gray zip-up and started back toward the school entrance. The halls weren't completely empty, but most of the kids who lingered after class had already retreated to their clubs or after-school practices. Security guards were beginning to direct anyone left to the cafeteria, but I ducked into the locker room instead. Luckily, the locker room led directly to the football field.

My earbuds were now secure in my pocket as I walked steadily past the locker wall, but the sounds of shuffling fabric got my attention, and I stopped. I didn't think anyone would be in here since I was definitely running late.

Curiosity got the best of me as I began twisting the combination to my locker. I didn't really care if someone else was here, but if by some slim chance it was Kyler, I was tempted to confirm it.

I pulled the locker door toward me, and the rustling noise stopped. There was a moment of silence before a deep voice echoed around the room. "Brynn?"

My hand twitched as I resisted the urge to slam it over my mouth. There was no way.

I'd acted on impulse opening the door, but now that he was actually here, I didn't know what to say. Luckily, Kyler couldn't see anything unless he bent down, which meant he couldn't see how bright my cheeks were turning.

Then I realized something. I'd never heard him say my name before.

"Oh, um," I mumbled. "Yeah. Sorry, are you in the middle of changing?" I wanted to slam my head into the locker. Of course he was. I didn't know why I'd asked that.

"Yeah," Kyler said. "Why? Do you want to watch?" Even though I couldn't see his face, I knew he wore a smug grin.

"No, thanks," I said immediately, closing the locker door on my side.

His laugh sounded like church bells with the way it resonated against steel lockers. "What are you doing in here?"

My back pressed against the shut door. "I'm hanging out with Liam after practice, so Adalia and I are waiting on the bleachers."

"Oh yeah? Well, make sure to watch me too," he said.

"Are you any good?"

"At football? Yeah, I'm good."

"I guess you'll have to prove it, then." I smiled, peeling myself off the locker wall. "I'll leave you alone now so you can change."

"You can stay longer," he replied.

"I don't want to distract you too much," I said, the grin still lingering on my lips. "See you in a minute."

"All right, fine," he replied with a light chuckle. "See you in a minute."

I walked to the door. The bright sun seemed blinding as I pushed open the handle, and I tried to shield my eyes. It only took a few seconds before they adjusted to the light, and I scanned the bleachers, looking for Adalia in the crowd of scattered girls.

She saw me before I saw her, and her arms flew up in an enthusiastic wave. "Brynn!"

Adalia sat in the front row with Liam and Sterling hanging off the fence that bordered the seats. Liam had one arm around the railing as he gestured with his spare hand, his practice jersey shifting as he did, and smiled at me. "Hurry up!" he called.

I was a little surprised to see Sterling with him, but Liam was the type who could make friends with anyone.

My pace quickened as I stepped up onto the bleachers and

took my place next to Adalia. "Hey," I said. "Sorry I'm late. I wasn't checking my phone."

"All good. I think our coach is waiting on Kyler, so we're running a little late," Liam said. "Oh, by the way, you know Sterling, right?"

"Yeah, we have history class together." I threw him a casual smile. "What's up?"

"Hey," he said. The sunlight made his bronze skin glimmer. Sterling looked at peace outside, with sun-kissed cheeks and the calm smile he always sent my way. "We were just talking about the project Mrs. Drella mentioned today."

"Thank God you came to interrupt," Liam said, dangling off the fence like a kid who'd just found a new playground. "I'm not even in that class and I'm bored."

I didn't even remember her mentioning a project, so I took Liam's cue and changed the subject. "You should have switched in while you still had the chance."

"You know what's weird, Brynn? I don't have a single class with you this year." He glanced at our bright-haired friend. "I'd rather have you than her. Adalia just uses me as a punching bag whenever she gets a question wrong, and I can only take so much." He sighed, and I could tell Adalia had to resist the urge to hit him over the fence. He grinned at her knowingly before shifting his eyes toward me. "I want to be in your class."

Sterling let out a laugh. "Our class is pretty chill, but that's probably 'cause everyone's half-asleep." His umber eyes flashed in my direction, resting on my face just a second too long. "What about you, Brynn? Do you like it?"

I blinked. "Oh, um, I guess—"

It suddenly became loud; the girls above us started talking with more excitement than before, and the four of us turned our heads in the same direction they were looking.

Kyler emerged from the boys' side of the locker room with a T-shirt and some sweats, but he hardly noticed that girls were trying to get his attention. His pale blue eyes seemed unfocused as he squinted away from the sun.

I hadn't been able to see his face in the locker room, but now that I was getting a better look, he seemed worn out. His brown hair was a mess, and prominent circles rested above his cheekbones. He stretched like a cat before throwing a lazy gaze toward the bleachers.

His eyes sparked for a moment when his gaze slid over mine, and he shot me a familiar grin.

The girls behind us squealed, but about half of them had their eyes glued to the black-haired boy in front of me, proving Adalia's theory that these two boys were the most popular at our school. I'm sure it tore the hearts of many as they had to decide who they liked better: Kyler, the mysterious bad boy with a radiating sense of confidence, or Sterling, the Prince Charming type who could sweep anyone off their feet with his smile.

Sterling shook his head with a slight grin, and when he caught me looking, he said, "Kyler's weird."

"What do you mean?" I asked.

"The rest of us are working our asses off, but he barely breaks a sweat until the game. He's a great player and, you know, my best friend, but I think he's over it. I mean, he just never seems like he's enjoying it anymore, so he always comes last minute,"

Sterling elaborated. "But I guess he knows our team would suffer if he quit."

I didn't know much about Kyler or his football abilities, but I remembered Liam saying something similar about how he was always late.

But if it was just that, why did he look so worn out?

Liam spoke up. "We should head over to the field now that he's here," he said, nudging Sterling.

"You're right. I'm really glad I got to talk to you guys." Sterling gave me a soft look. Then the two boys jumped off the platform. Sterling caught up to Kyler with a playful tackle and ruffled his hair while Liam laughed as he walked at their side.

After he was gone, Adalia slid her hands around my arm and snuggled in closer. Her green eyes crinkled as she glanced up and gave a cheeky grin. "Sterling was totally looking at you."

So I hadn't imagined it.

Sure he'd given me a couple of looks, but I hadn't thought much of it. I mean, we'd never really talked until today, so it couldn't mean anything.

"Sterling's nice to everyone. He was probably just trying to make me feel included since I came late."

"Hmm, maybe," Adalia said skeptically. A couple beats of silence passed before she spoke again. Her words were soft, hesitant. "You know, I heard something about Ingrid." I tensed as I turned in her direction, but Adalia was facing forward, her eyes focused on the field in front of us. "I just thought you might want to hear it, but if it's going to make you feel worse—"

"No!" I said, a little too loudly. When a few people glanced in our direction, I gave an awkward cough and started again, this time quieter. "I mean, no, it won't make me feel worse. What's up?"

"It's nothing much. I just heard some people talking in one of my classes, and I guess someone who knew Ingrid was saying that she was having issues with her parents or something before the accident. A couple of them thought that the whole tripping thing seemed weird, too, so I just wanted you to know that you're not alone in thinking something might be going on."

Adalia was looking at me now, her eyes searching my face for a reaction. I didn't know how to react, but I knew that she'd told me so I would feel better and maybe less crazy about wanting to get justice for Ingrid.

My arms wrapped around her neck as I went in for a hug. "Thanks, Ad. Thanks for looking out for me."

When I pulled back, we were both smiling.

"We're in this together," Adalia said. "I wish I could tell you more, but that's all I've heard so far."

I shook my head. "It's enough."

SO I WAS A LITTLE LATE.

Big deal, I thought to myself, my grip tightening on the steering wheel. There was hardly any traffic, since school had started half an hour ago, but that didn't stop me from following the speed limit like a respectable, do-gooder teenage girl.

My heart jumped every time my eyes glanced at the digital clock, laughing at me for being such an idiot. I always, *always* remembered to set an alarm before I went to sleep. But last night, when I had closed my eyes to the droning sound of the television in front of me, I hadn't been thinking about preparing for the next day.

I was just happy to get some sleep.

Sleep used to come easily, but after stumbling across the scene of Ingrid's death, my sleep pattern had taken a turn for the worse. I couldn't close my eyes without seeing blond hair with blood seeping through the strands. I'd tried not to look at her face that night, but my eyes hadn't listened, and the quick glimpse I'd caught flashed through my mind whenever I tried to sleep, churning and twisting her features into something so gruesome I had no choice but to wake up.

It was miserable, but I had no reason to feel sorry for myself. Not when she was dead and I was alive. I'd replayed that night over and over in my head, trying to figure out what I could have done differently so that the next day we were both at school, laughing with our friends, hating on the cafeteria food, doing homework. Maybe I should have walked faster. Maybe I shouldn't have delayed my arrival by calling Baylor first. I should have run straight there when I heard the scream.

I hadn't done any of that. Now I had to live with my potentially fatal mistake.

I tried to snap out of it as I turned in to the mostly full parking lot. I parked in the back and hauled myself out of the white Jeep, swinging my backpack on before I slammed the door closed and ran. Unsurprisingly, I didn't make it very far before another setback stopped me, except this time, it was in the form of a human being. "Excuse me," I muttered without looking up. A frown was etched onto my face as I tried to walk past whoever it was before they moved in the same direction I did, and suddenly,

I snapped my gaze up. "Seriously? Look, I've had a really bad morning, so if you could just—"

"In a hurry?" Kyler chortled, and for a second, all I could do was stare. Of course I'd run into Kyler, and he would have that cocky grin on his lips, completely oblivious to the state of panic I was in.

I was never late to school, and it wasn't a big deal, but it just seemed like everything had been going wrong since Ingrid.

He pushed open the door in front of me, waving me inside as if he had suddenly transformed into an usher. With a small sigh, I walked past him before he was next to me, his body towering over mine.

"So," he asked after a few steps, "did I impress you?"

I blinked at him before I remembered the conversation we'd had in the locker room.

"You were all right," I answered, trying my best to sound indifferent. To be honest, I didn't know much about football, although it was always fun cheering in the student section. Aside from that, I wasn't really qualified to judge who was good or bad at it.

He grinned. "Just all right?"

"Well." My head turned in his direction. I tried to remember what I'd seen, but the only things I could recall were his arms. They were toned, and when he threw the ball or flexed, I'd had to try extrahard not to stare. "I think you throw pretty well," I finally said.

Kyler gave me a knowing grin. "So, you were watching me."

I rolled my eyes. Of course he was teasing me.

"Don't you ever get tired of flirting, Kyler?" I asked lightly, focusing my attention elsewhere when his hand gently brushed against my wrist.

"Not if it's with you."

His blue eyes almost shone when I looked back in surprise, and for a moment, I couldn't tear my gaze away. Tousled brown hair gave him a messy look, but it wasn't wild. It was soft, just like his expression.

My lips remained parted before Kyler added, "But if you don't like it, I'll stop."

Did I like it? To be honest, I didn't think much of it. It was kind of fun to hear what he could come up with.

His face didn't hurt, either.

"I don't hate it," I decided.

He gave a shy smile before cocking his head toward the main office. As we approached the desk, he stood next to me with heavy eyes while I asked for my pass. I felt the weight of his gaze on me, and that, along with the already unsettled feelings I associated with this office, made a mess out of my nerves. I decided to leave just as quickly as I'd come. I didn't wait for Kyler. It wasn't like I needed to, and once I had the pass in my hand, I was heading for the door and . . .

Tripping.

An arm wrapped around my waist to stop me from total humiliation. "Wow, Brynn. Are you falling for me?" Kyler asked, taking his time as he removed his hand. Warmth slid against my midriff, his touch lingering ever so softly as he let me go.

My heart began to race until I actually processed what he'd said. I snorted. "Seriously?" I asked, looking directly into his eyes. "That's the best you could come up with?"

He blinked back at me. "It was the first thing I thought of. Fine. Give me a minute, I'll think of something better just for you." He quickly went back to the desk to get his own pass, and then he was back in the hallway with me.

We walked side by side for a little longer, though he seemed lost in thought as he tried to come up with something clever. I took the chance and let my gray eyes peek up, wondering what kind of expression he was making.

He caught my eye.

I hurriedly bit my cheek and glanced anywhere else but his face.

I'd almost forgotten about the bright pink slip in front of me, and I held it out, pretending to examine it so that I wouldn't get trapped by any of his questioning looks.

As we reached a familiar room, I gave him a slight nod. "That's my class."

Kyler followed my gaze before looking back at me with a glint in his eyes. I gave him a confused look before he brought his finger up to the bottom of his eye.

"You've got a lash," he said.

"What?" I answered quickly, my hand racing up to my own cheek. I still didn't know Kyler all that well, which meant it was nerve-wracking enough to walk alone by his side. If he was serious, and I'd actually had an eyelash there the entire time, I never wanted to face him again.

"Did I get it?" I mumbled after fumbling around with my hand.

"Closer to the right."

"Your right?"

"My left," he said with a slight grin on his lips.

"This isn't helping," I replied, a little frustrated.

"Can I?" he asked, his voice suddenly taking on a low edge. When I gave a small nod, Kyler leaned down slowly, easily, before I felt his thumb run softly across the skin under my eye. I couldn't help but stare at the way his lashes fanned against ice-blue eyes.

Then he moved closer to my face, and I could make out the faint brush of his lips against my ear. His breath felt cool, and suddenly the blood in my veins turned hot. "Just kidding," he whispered. "But—"

We both heard the footsteps at the same time as we turned in unison to see a girl walking down the hall. She might've made eye contact with me, but her head was looking down before I had time to be sure. Kyler stood up, pulling his face away, and a gust of cool air hit my cheeks.

Once she was out of view, Kyler's grin stretched wide. "That was better, right?"

"Oh my God, Kyler," I said, appalled. He'd done all that just because I'd laughed at his earlier pickup line? I brought my hands up to my warm face once his back was turned to me. "That was unfair."

"All's fair in love and war," he replied, a chuckle lingering in his words.

Then he was gone, and I stood flustered and extralate for class.

"NICE OF YOU TO JOIN US," Mrs. Drella said as I finally came into the classroom. I'd tried to compose myself a little, but I knew my face was still flushed. I did my best to ignore it as I handed her the pink slip.

"Sorry," I mumbled. She sat at her desk, her glasses sitting on the end of her nose as she looked at the pass.

"You missed my explanation regarding the project, so you'll be responsible for catching up," she said. She threw the slip into a drawer and gestured to the desks behind me. "Find a group to work with."

Adalia caught my eye immediately; her hand waved me toward her under the desk. Her desk was pushed together with two others, one belonging to Sterling and the other to a brown-haired boy named Jayden. I only knew his name because Adalia had thought he was cute freshman year.

"Hey, guys," I said, sliding my backpack off my shoulder and dropping it near my chair. My fingers dug under the desk as I dragged it next to Adalia's and plopped into the seat. "Sorry I'm late."

"I think you said that at practice too," Sterling said with a gentle smile. Creases formed by his lips. "I hope you don't mind working with us. We thought it would be easy to just turn our desks around."

"Oh, that's totally fine," I said, pulling out my notebook and pencil case. There were four packets on the table, and I slid one toward me. "What are we doing?"

Jayden spoke up. "It's just some research project. We have to make a board about whoever she assigned to us."

"We got Al Capone," Adalia said. She held up a paper with his picture printed on the front, and my eyes went wide.

"Wasn't he a gangster?"

"Yeah," Sterling replied. "But I think he's more interesting than some of the other options."

"You're right." Jayden laughed.

Once we split up the work, deciding who was going to do which part of the assignment, I began to feel my focus drift. My thoughts kept leading me back to Kyler and how flustered he'd made me earlier. To be honest, I didn't have much experience with guys. Actually, I didn't have any.

There had been a boy in fifth grade that I'd kind of liked, but I told him we couldn't date until I was in high school. He said he'd wait for me, which was romantic at the time, but when I saw him again in middle school at a basketball game, I avoided him.

I know, I know, I'm a horrible person. I couldn't help it.

I also couldn't help provoking Kyler. His teasing was kind of fun, but the unfortunate fact was that I was no match for him. Sure, I was acting like I could handle it, but in reality, there was no way I'd be immune to his touches or his warm gaze.

". . . and then we can do this part together. Sound good?" Adalia's dreamy voice trailed back into focus. Green eyes blinked at me. "Brynn?"

"What? Sorry. I got distracted for a second, but I'm fine with anything."

Adalia placed the back of her hand against my cheek. "Your face seems kind of warm. Do you have a cold?" Then she grinned sneakily. "Or were you thinking about someone?"

My eyes grew wide, and she laughed, knowing just how spot-on she was. "I'll tell you later," I mumbled, attempting to concentrate on the assignment at hand. But just when I had finally begun to process the words on the pages, the bell ending class rang out.

Before waving bye to Adalia, I stepped out of the classroom, trying to ignore the spot outside the door where I'd been with Kyler just a short while ago. When I got to my next class, there weren't too many people there yet, mostly because my last period was pretty close to this one. But when Kyler walked in, whispers suddenly began swirling around me.

It wasn't like it was unusual for girls to whisper, but the fact that most of them kept looking at me as they talked was a little concerning.

I tried to ignore it, but it was hard. The sound of light foot-steps coming from behind got my attention, and I turned in that direction, watching as a group of girls approached Kyler's desk. Their attempts at flirting were priceless as they followed the cliché of batting eyelashes and twirling hair, giving Kyler admiring looks. He didn't seem to mind the atten-tion, and I tore my gaze away.

"Hey, Ky," a brown-haired girl said. Her voice sounded almost sultry as she continued, "So, I heard you're going out with someone."

I found myself eavesdropping as he responded, "Oh? Who's the lucky girl?"

I couldn't help but laugh when the words left his lips, and I quickly rushed to cover my mouth with my hand. Hopefully they hadn't heard me, yet the silence that followed might have been an indicator they had. The girl continued in a deeper voice. "Brynn. But it's not true, right? I mean, you would never get serious with a girl."

"Who knows?" he said.

What?

I quickly twisted in my seat, my body facing sideways as I met his coy eyes in disbelief. When he chuckled, the girls gave me glares that could kill, so I answered for him. "We're not dating."

"Don't be like that," Kyler purred as he rested his cheek on his hand. "There's nothing wrong with admitting it."

I tried frowning, but laughter teased my lips instead. Shaky corners lifted, and I looked at the girls. "Who told you we're dating?"

Kyler followed my gaze as a different one spoke up. "Well, I mean, a lot of people. You were both late this morning, right? Some girl saw you in the hall together, like, kissing or something? I don't know. But everyone is talking about it."

I threw a vicious look at Kyler, who conveniently became interested in something else. I was about to reply, but the bell starting class rang loudly, and everyone strode back to their seats.

Our teacher came strutting in with a bright smile on her lips. "Good morning, class."

I wasn't sure what word I would've used, but *good* wasn't one of them.

CHAPTER FIVE

"So, I have a really important question," Adalia said later that day. Her voice was barely audible over the loud noises of the cafeteria around us, and suddenly, I was starting to regret not hiding out in some quieter classroom for lunch. Her hand hovered over the science worksheet that was due next period before she set the pencil down firmly. When Liam and I looked up at her with expectant gazes, she continued, gesturing at the paper, "How is this relevant?"

Liam shrugged. "It doesn't have to be relevant. It's the school system. Pass our classes. Go to college. The end."

She groaned, frowning at her sheet of incomplete homework. "But I'm not going to be a scientist! I don't even remember what we did last week!"

"Yeah, me neither. Sorry, Ad." I tried to sympathize with her, but Liam had a point. Then again, so did she. "We can change the school system later."

She averted her eyes and continued to mumble something about our chemistry teacher being a jackass. Adalia and Liam had the same class next period, but mine was toward the end of the day. With a slight smile, I looked over my own home-work. I'd gotten more done than she had, but Liam's paper was tucked somewhere in his mess of a backpack. He was smarter than most of the people I knew, though he didn't come off that way at first glance. It was one of the things I liked about him. When I gave him a curious look, he leaned back and placed his hands behind his head.

"Hey, I've got a football scholarship. As long as I don't get a D, I'm good."

"I want a scholarship," Adalia grumbled, then she let out a long, exasperated sigh. She loved to be dramatic. "This isn't fair. You're good at science, Li! Can you help us?"

I nodded in agreement, and, in unison, we gazed at him with puppy dog eyes. "Please?"

He looked over his shoulder and away from us. With his eyes closed, he hit his face with his palm. "Why am I so nice? What did I do to deserve your endless torture?"

Adalia pushed herself up from her chair and leaned over the table. Her face was close to his. "Is that a yes? You'll help us?"

He opened an eye, then, before she had time to react, he reached over and used both of his hands to ruffle Adalia's hair. She let out a small shriek when he laughed, and then he nodded. "Yeah, I'll help you guys."

"I can't believe you did that!" she exclaimed, and he sepa-rated his long legs so that a part of his chair was vacant for her.

"I'll fix it. Come here," he said playfully, and, after a moment of hesitation, she went over to his side. "Could you check my calendar and tell me when I have practices? We should pick a day to study."

She grabbed his phone from the table, using her thumb to unlock it, and began scrolling through his schedules. As he played with her hair, he looked over at me with a grin. "By the way, Brynn, I heard an interesting rumor this morning."

I raised my eyebrows and choked out, "Oh no."

"Looks like someone's got a boyfriend," he said in a singsong voice, and Adalia's head shot up like a spring.

"What? A boyfriend?" She gawked at me. "Who is it?"

I opened my mouth to respond, but someone else spoke first. "Me."

His low voice made my heart freeze.

I didn't have to look behind me to know who it was, as the expressions Liam and Adalia wore were explanation enough. Liam's mouth began to curve into a grin, but Adalia seemed dumbstruck as her eyes jumped from me to Kyler then back to me.

"What?" Adalia trilled. "Oh my God."

"Wait, Ad—" I started.

"Kyler?" another voice said, and this time I did turn around. His best friend's black hair fell above his eyes when he looked down at me, and Sterling's confused expression turned into a smile. "Hey."

"What are you guys doing here?" Liam gave them a wide smile, probably excited to see his teammates. "I thought you never ate in the cafeteria."

Sterling's face fell back into confusion, and he glanced at Kyler for some type of answer. "We usually don't," Sterling began, "but he started walking in here, so I guess I just kind of followed."

Kyler's eyes caught mine as he looked down at me and grinned. "I wanted to eat lunch with my girlfriend."

I tore my gaze away, focusing instead on the lunch laid out in front of me. "You're ridiculous," I said, doing my best to keep calm. I peeked upward timidly. "But you can sit with us if you want."

Kyler's smile seemed childlike now, and I almost preferred it over the way his lips usually twisted in a knowing manner. He slid into the seat next to me, his arm just barely tapping mine. Sterling sat across from him.

"Adalia," I said. Her eyes sparkled as if she were watching a show unfold, and I laughed. "We're not actually dating. It's just a misunderstanding. And—" Kyler leaned forward, his voice whispering in my ear. "Yeah, sure," I said back to Kyler. Then I turned toward Adalia and continued. "But yeah, we're not dating."

Liam rested his cheek against his palm, shaking his head. "Misunderstanding, huh? You're going to tell us that and then flirt right in front of my salad?"

"What? Flirt?" I asked.

"He just whispered in your ear! Right in front of us!" Liam pointed toward Kyler, who'd just stuffed one of my fries in his face, with an accusing finger.

My face reddened until I resembled one of Liam's tomatoes. "I'm so sorry, I didn't even realize . . . he just asked me for a fry." My head flicked in Kyler's direction. "You baited me."

"Maybe."

I shook my head. "Anyway, the point is that we're not dating," I said with finality. Adalia gave a slight "Mmhmm," but the rest of the table went back to having their own conversations, and the focus was no longer on me.

"Seriously, though." I faced Kyler again. "What should we do about the rumors?"

He looked unbothered. His hoodie creased as he slanted his body toward me and shrugged. "It's up to you, Brynn."

"You're having fun with it, aren't you?"

He gave a sheepish grin. "Is it that obvious?"

"Yes. Are you bored?"

Kyler let out a breathy laugh before his gaze caught on my hand. He reached out and ran his thumb across my knuckles before smirking. "Maybe I actually like you."

"It's only been a week since we had our first conversation," I said, my eyes trailing our fingers as he began to intertwine them. He did it so naturally, so idly, that I could barely resist. "So I don't believe you."

Blue eyes dared mine.

"Then I guess we'll have to change that."

KYLER AND STERLING LEFT before the three of us did. Apparently, they had to get to their class a little early.

With their absence, I would've expected it to feel more relaxed, more natural, but something about the atmosphere was off-putting. Liam sat quietly, munching on an apple slice as he ran his hand through his short, dark hair. His eyes kept flickering back to Adalia, and that's when I realized what it was.

Her lips were downturned.

"Adalia?" I asked, and she snapped out of any daze she was in.

She gave a faltering smile when she replied.

"Yeah?"

I frowned. "What's wrong?"

Her usually shining green eyes were dull as she looked down, and I felt ashamed that I hadn't noticed it earlier. Maybe she hadn't been showing it with Kyler and Sterling around, but now that it was just the three of us, she was letting her facade slip.

She seemed to contemplate whether or not she was ready to share. Then she shook her head. "It's nothing big. I just got into an argument with my dad last night, and having to do this point-less homework is making everything feel worse."

Liam nodded and crossed his arms. They were naturally tanned, but all the time he spent at practice had made them even darker. "Science sucks."

Adalia's smile seemed a little brighter at his effort to agree. "It does."

"What did you get into an argument about?" I asked. If she'd been willing to bring it up in the first place, I hoped talking about it would make her feel better.

"Money," she said in an exasperated tone. "You'd think he'd know better. He's the adult."

Adalia lived with her dad. Her parents had gotten divorced when she was young; her mom had moved to Missouri, and Adalia chose to stay here with her dad. I'd met him a thou-sand times, and he was fun to be around, but we all knew he could be a bit immature sometimes. Adalia hated having to be the responsible one, and I didn't think it was fair of him to expect that from her.

"You shouldn't have to babysit him," I murmured. "I'm sorry, Ad. It's unfair."

"Yeah," she said. "I was looking through our account, just to see how much I could spend on groceries this month, you know, nothing big . . . but it was bad. Like worse than it's ever been."

"What did he say about it?" Liam asked, his eyes alert.

She shrugged. "He acted like it was fine. Said it was a one-time thing. I want to believe him, but . . . we ended up arguing, and now it's kind of awkward."

"You can always stay at my place," I suggested.

Liam perked up. "Mine too. My brothers love you."

Adalia laughed. Thinking about his two younger brothers must have lifted her spirits. "Thanks, guys. It's fine. I'm going to talk to him again and make it less uncomfortable."

Liam's expression was so soft that I almost wanted to look away. We both must have thought the same thing: Adalia was admirable. She was always looking out for others, but she knew how to handle her own problems too.

"Okay," I said with a nod. "You got this."

"I got this," she repeated.

CHAPTER SIX

THE REST OF THAT WEEK WAS SLOW. The weekend wasn't as full and exciting as the last one; I'd talked to my parents again, but they didn't have many updates aside from the specifics of their coding progression. Adalia and Liam had come over a couple times, and Baylor teased me for not being able to make any new friends.

Something about what Adalia had told us continued to bother me, though. It wasn't just the fact that I was upset as her friend, but it sounded similar to what she'd mentioned about Ingrid. Ingrid hadn't been getting along with her parents before the accident, and I was more curious now as to why.

Had it also been money problems?

It could have been anything, but I couldn't shake the feeling that something was off.

Now it was Monday, and I was stressing out during second period not only because of Adalia but also because of something dumb.

For some reason, Kyler always came into second period just

before the bell rang. I was the opposite. Since my last class wasn't too far away, I usually found myself among the first five students to arrive. It wasn't like I was waiting for Kyler or anything, but the anticipation of seeing him come through the door always made me fidget awkwardly in my seat, desperately searching for things to do on my phone.

It was like going up on a roller coaster, and the drop was the way he'd look at me with his sky-blue eyes or smirk like he could read all my thoughts.

I wanted to make him feel that way too. I wanted his stomach to drop and his face to flush because of me.

I suddenly felt his heavy gaze and peeked up from my phone, just enough that I saw him casually stride toward our row. His cuffed blue jeans only emphasized how tall he was; I was never going to ask his exact height, but I knew I was five feet, five inches and had to look up when we spoke. My eyes lined up just below his chin when I stood next to him, but luckily his height had nothing on me when we both sat at our desks.

He grinned as he walked past, and I gave a slight nod in return. I hadn't expected him to talk to me, and yet I was surprised at the tinge of disappointment that bit when he didn't.

Only a minute passed before I felt a tap on my shoulder. My head barely began to turn before that tap turned into a gentle hand pulling me backward in my seat, and his face turned up next to me.

"You look pretty today, Brynn." Kyler's voice was entrancing— low and hoarse and sweet all at once. I turned farther to gawk at him in surprise, but he gave a youthful laugh and looked at me with mischievous eyes. "Your cheeks are turning red."

My hands flew to my face as I spun forward and tried to disappear. It was only second period, and I was already acting like a fool because of him.

The increasingly loud clanking sound of high heels on the ground appeared, and the whole class glanced up in unison. Mrs. Johnson was our second-period teacher and a more favored option. She was laid back, young, and always tried to make classes fun.

She smiled at us, her rosy cheeks looking brighter as the classroom lights reflected off them. "Today we're doing partner worksheets," she said, pushing a wave of auburn hair behind her shoulder. "I'll be passing them back, so move your desks together with whoever you want to work with."

Kyler tapped my shoulder again. "Want to be partners?" he asked, making sure it was loud enough for the rest of the class to hear.

"Maybe. Are you good at psychology?" I asked, trying to seem as cool as possible to overwrite the way I'd blushed a few minutes ago.

"Totally. You can even ask Mrs. Johnson," he said. His hand suddenly rose into the air. "I'm good at this class, right, Mrs. Johnson?"

The overdramatic gesture caught Mrs. Johnson's attention as her eyes flicked toward mine then back to Kyler. Her lips broke out into a charmed smile. "You are when you try."

"Thank you," Kyler said, his eyes flashing in amusement at the situation he'd put me in. "See? I'll try. For you."

I guessed there wasn't a reason to say no. "Okay," I agreed. "We can work together."

The desks had all been pushed together in pairs, and as Kyler sat across from me, his intense stare never leaving my face, it was hard to pay attention to what I was writing on the worksheet. Finally, I huffed and threw a soft glare his way. "How long are you going to stare?"

"I can't help it," he drawled, and I ignored him as I pushed the paper in his direction.

"She wants us to write about the bystander effect. So, what do you think?" I asked, tapping a pen against my chin. I always enjoyed learning about psychological phenomena, and ideas were already beginning to swim in my head. It almost made me forget who my partner was as I continued, "Which part should we focus on?"

"Which part do you think is the most interesting?"

I had to think about that. "Mrs. Johnson said that you should help in ways that don't endanger yourself."

"Right," Kyler said, his focus on me. His silence provoked me into elaborating.

"So . . . how far do you go?" I inquired.

"I guess it depends. In the examples she gave us, they're talking about helping strangers out. I don't know how far I'd go for someone I didn't know. I probably wouldn't endanger myself," Kyler said.

His words made me think about Ingrid.

I hadn't known her. Not really. I'd just been in the wrong place at the wrong time, but that didn't excuse me for not being able to help. "I think the guilt of not helping when you could would make me help." I paused, replaying my sentence in my head. "Did that make sense? Like, if I knew I could help someone and

I didn't, I'd feel bad. So I'd rather just help than continue to feel bad."

Kyler chuckled. "That made sense."

"But what about you? You said you wouldn't endanger yourself for strangers, but what if you knew them?"

"Then I would," he said automatically, "if it was someone close to me or someone I cared about. Wouldn't anyone?"

"I don't know," I said. "There are all those songs that talk about taking a bullet for someone, but is it that easy? I don't expect anyone to be able to put me before themselves."

"There's not always a gun," he said. "I think endangering yourself for the sake of others can mean a lot of things. You can do it a lot of different ways."

"Yeah?" I asked.

"Yeah," Kyler repeated. "Like blowing up at the school psychiatrist and risking getting expelled." He gave me a wink, and my lips quivered into a small smile.

It had been for the sake of Ingrid, but also for the sake of everyone else. For the sake of our safety. Yet, I would admit there were probably better ways to go about it than yelling at Denise the salad shaker. "You're never going to let me live that down, are you?" I asked, the smile lingering on my lips.

"Never," he confirmed. Kyler looked up at the clock then back toward the paper. "So then, I guess our conclusion is that our level of endangerment relies on the person in question."

Although it wasn't a groundbreaking revelation, it was enough for this class.

"Perfect," I said.

He held my gaze a little longer than usual before I averted

my eyes. I pulled over the worksheet and began writing about what we'd discussed. "Wait," Kyler said, slim fingers grazing the top of the paper. "I'll do the rest."

His handwriting contrasted with the way he talked; his words were spoken like silk laced with mischief, but his handwriting seemed youthful, with loopier letters and a distinctive pattern. I knew it wasn't much, but learning more about him made me feel satisfied.

Even if it was just his handwriting.

"Brynn," he said. I hadn't noticed he'd stopped writing, and I looked up.

"Yeah?"

"What are you doing tonight?"

My eyes blinked. *Huh*?

The thumping of my heart became louder as I realized what he meant. I tried not to stammer as I peered back at him with a fake calm. "Nothing. Why?"

"Do you want to go on a date?" Kyler's gaze was unwavering as he scanned my face. My parted lips felt vulnerable as his eyelids dropped, leaving only a slit of sultry blue. "I can pick you up after practice."

He was being serious. "Sure," I squeaked, surprising even myself. I cleared my throat. "I mean, yeah. Okay. What do you want to do?"

"What about dinner? What kind of food do you like?"

I began running through a mental list of restaurants in town before quickly hitting the brakes. Was I actually doing this? Was this actually happening? Never in my wildest dreams had I imagined going on a date with Kyler. And yeah, he thought that pretending to date was funny, but he didn't have to go this far.

I recalled our first lunch. He couldn't have been serious about liking me, right? There was no way.

But if, by some tiny chance, he was serious, what would I do? Did I like him? It didn't seem impossible.

But still, he was Kyler. He had fans. He liked to flirt as a hobby. Was he really someone I wanted to be vulnerable with?

I glanced up to see him leaning on the desk, his cheek resting in his palm with a lazy smile as he watched me. "I know," he teased. "It's a hard decision."

He didn't know the half of it.

"What about sushi?" Was sushi too much for a first date? Were there going to be more? These thoughts were becoming overwhelming.

"Sounds good," he said. "I'll pick you up at seven."

IT WAS SIX-THIRTY, and my nerves were beginning to feel like a sickness. I tried to focus on the mirror in front of me, double-checking for any smears of mascara or strands of hair sticking out. A pale face stared back at me with eyebrows creased in uncomfortable anticipation.

I brushed against the beauty mark under my eye and peered up. At least my eyelashes seemed all right; they arched up in a dark flare, which reflected the general theme of my appearance. Everything was dark and muted. Smoky gray eyes, which only my mother seemed to pull off, and dusky, desaturated hair. Loose strands sprung like a frame around my face, and I bobbed my head to watch a curled ponytail bounce along behind.

Now it was a quarter to seven.

My stomach felt filled with bees, humming and stinging as I pushed up from the chair in my room. I'd expected to be a little nervous. It was my first date ever, and, to make it even more nerve-wracking, it was with Kyler. He'd probably know exactly what to do as I fumbled around, making a fool out of myself with tomato-red cheeks.

At least I didn't need to wear much blush.

I trailed down the stairs, my steps light compared to the weight I felt, and wandered around the kitchen. I threw a look at the door across the living room. Kyler was going to be here in fifteen—no—ten minutes now. What would I say? What was he wearing?

He'd told me to wear a dress, and luckily, I had a few. It'd taken me about an hour of trying them all on a few times, and with helpful input from Adalia over FaceTime, we'd decided that a form-fitting burgundy dress was the winner. I wore simple lace-up heels to match, but I didn't know if that was too much. Maybe it was too little. I was stressed.

Now there were five minutes left.

I hated this feeling. I hoped he was struggling as much as I was, but I doubted it. He was probably singing along to music in his car without a care in the world as I paced the floor next to my door. My eye caught on a puffy black jacket slung from the couch's back, and I grabbed it just as the doorbell rang.

Suddenly, I couldn't breathe.

My heart overtook my ears, its pace matching the quick steps I took as I opened the door to reveal Kyler's lopsided smirk.

"Hey." His familiar voice almost gave me relief.

He wore a sleek button-up, folded just below his elbows and tucked into dark gray pants. Just the top button was undone, and I hastily brushed my eyes past. The outfit gave him a statue-like silhouette, outlining a broad chest and slimmer waist. His pants cut just above his ankles, and I finally snapped my head up.

"Hey," I repeated. The black silk of his shirt matched the inky sky behind us, which was littered with winking stars and a bright full moon.

"I know I already said this today," he started, "but you look pretty."

"So do you."

A dimple creased his cheek. "Thanks. I tried." Kyler nodded toward a black car parked in front of the house. "Ready to go?"

It was embarrassing to admit, but seeing his calm face and familiar grin eased my nerves. The past hour of hell seemed like a dream now, and my stomach was no longer doing twirls.

"Yeah." I smiled as I followed him out my front door. He opened the car door for me, and I slid into a leather seat.

"It's really close," he said. And it was. About five minutes later, we were pulling into a large parking lot next to a modern-looking building with dark wooden pillars and a sleek logo shining at the top. Glass walls hinted at the atmosphere inside, with a multitude of colors coming from the champagne and wine bottles on display at the bar.

"C'mon." The lights reflected off Kyler's face as he held out his hand and helped me to my feet.

As we entered the restaurant, I could almost smell how luxurious it was. I'd let Kyler pick the place, but I hadn't really expected him to pick a place like this. Now that we were inside, my nerves threatened to resurface.

"Kyler," I whispered uncomfortably as someone from behind took my jacket. I nodded to them as a token of appreciation before turning my head back to him. "This place is, um, kind of expensive, isn't it?"

"It's fine. I'm paying." He waved his hand dismissively as if it wasn't a big deal. Except that it totally was.

I followed quietly as the host showed us to our booth, letting my gaze wander around the tables set with candles and flowers. The lights were dimmed, and the dull buzz of chatter was soft.

I slid into my seat as Kyler took the one opposite me, and once the host left, his eyes skimmed over me with amusement.

"Like it?" he asked, though I knew he was searching for my reaction. How should I have acted? Thrilled? Ecstatic? Maybe a little impressed?

"It's nice," I replied, doing my best to shield any hints at my thoughts. He rose an eyebrow at me, and I continued with a trace of a smile. "It almost makes me forget that we're both high school students who find spare change in our cars."

The corner of his lip lifted in reply, then he was looking at the menu, raising his glance a few times in an attempt to meet mine. "What are you getting?"

"I don't know," I sighed, squinting at the menu. Everything was so expensive, with different types of seafood and additions I'd never tasted before. I knew sushi was normally on the pricey side, but this place seemed to take pride in its extravagance. "Maybe the California roll?"

Kyler gave an unimpressed look. "That's the cheapest thing here."

"Yeah, but . . ." My words trailed off as I searched for something else.

"Hey," Kyler said, his hand brushing the top of mine. His gaze was gentle as he peered at me. "If I wanted you to get something like that, I would've brought you to a different place. Seriously. Get something you want, or else I'm going to order extra food and your efforts to save my wallet will be meaningless."

I couldn't help but feel touched by his words. The place was overwhelming for sure, but he'd eased my doubts in just a few sentences, and for that, I was grateful. "You're ridiculous," I finally said, my eyes crinkling. "Fine. I'll get something really fancy, and you can't complain."

"That's the spirit."

I revisited the menu in a new light, now wondering what butter ponzu was and if it would taste good with crab claw tempura. The rest of the menu was as much of a mystery, but luckily, I had the internet.

I glanced at Kyler. There was no look of panic in his eyes, and he seemed in his element as his gaze shifted down the menu. Kyler's familiarity with the place raised some suspicion, and I couldn't help myself as I blurted, "So, is this where you normally take girls?"

His eyes widened before he coughed down a laugh, and at my confused expression, he said with a lingering smile, "Am I known for bringing girls on dates?"

I shrugged my shoulders, hoping I didn't sound bitter. "Well,

I mean, you're known for flirting with them, right? Fancy dinners generally impress girls."

"So you're impressed?"

"You didn't answer the question," I responded, hardly sparing him a glance as a server appeared at the edge of our table. Kyler followed my gaze, and a man dressed in black and white smiled at us.

"How are you guys doing? I'm Andy, and I'll be your server tonight. I see you already got some water, so if you're ready, I can take your orders now." He looked at Kyler, and I felt relieved I didn't have to go first.

"Thanks." Kyler smiled. "Can I get the eel sashimi and the crab tempura?"

"Of course." Andy turned his head to me. "And you?"

I blinked. "Can I get the same thing as him without the sashimi?"

Kyler's eyes found mine, and he smirked.

"Yes! Will that be all?" Andy asked.

"Yes. Thank you," I said. He continued scribbling in his notepad as he scurried away, and I almost wished he'd stayed so that I didn't have to face Kyler and his knowing looks.

"I was already going to order that, by the way," I mumbled, turning my face away. I knew I shouldn't have been embarrassed, but I was.

Kyler let out a low laugh. "I wasn't thinking otherwise. I guess we have similar taste. And Brynn," he started, propelling my gaze back up, "I don't take girls on dates. So you don't need to be jealous."

He threw a sly smile from across the table.

"I wasn't jealous," I said quickly. My fingers fumbled together under the table. "I was just curious." With a shy upward glance, I added quietly, "I don't really know much about you."

"Yeah," he said. "Me neither. That's why I wanted to hang out."

My face flushed in the dark. "What do you want to know?"

He hummed as his fingers began flipping one of the forks over. He suddenly stopped and looked back at me. "What kind of things do you like to do when you're not at school?"

"Like hobbies?"

He nodded.

I tried to resist laughing. It was a normal question to ask on a first date, but it seemed almost too innocent to come out of Kyler's mouth. "I guess I like cooking. I'm not very good at it yet, but sometimes my brother will taste test things for me. He's only complained once, but that was because I made something too spicy."

"Your brother's Baylor, right?"

"Yeah." I was a little surprised. "How'd you know?"

"He was a senior on the football team when I was a freshman. He was really good."

"You know, I've heard that you're really good at football, too, but you don't like it that much so you're always late to practice," I said.

His eyebrows rose. "Oh yeah?" He paused. "I guess I don't love it, but that's not why I'm late all the time."

"Liam thinks it's because you're busy with girls."

"What about you?" Kyler asked, his eyes flashing in amusement as he teased me. "What do you think?"

"I don't know," I said, trying to fake indifference.

Kyler's smile widened. "You're cute. And since you're cute, I'll tell you the real reason. My deep, dark secret."

"Oh?" I asked, now intrigued. I'd been wondering.

"It's not that interesting, though. I go back home after school to try and help around the house," Kyler said. He spoke about it as if it were a fact and nothing more. "Since my dad passed away, my mom has been working a lot more. Not that she needs to. She already makes enough, but I think it's her way of coping. So I try to make things a little easier for her while she's gone by doing the dishes and vacuuming, simple things like that."

My mind drew a blank at what to say. It wasn't something I'd expected, but I didn't know what to expect when it came to him. I did know one thing, though, and that was the more I learned about him, the more I seemed to like him.

I couldn't think of an appropriate thing to say, so I ended up saying something dumb.

"You know how to vacuum?"

Kyler's eyes widened just a bit before he laughed. "Yeah," he said, his grin wide. "I do."

"Wow," I said. "Now I'm impressed."

"That's what sold it for you, huh?"

I nodded. "So you're not late because you hate football?"

"Nah," he said. "I don't love it, but it's too late to quit now. I've been playing since I was a freshman."

I tried to recall the games I used to go to when Baylor was there, but I couldn't remember Kyler anywhere. "Were you good then?"

"No," he said with a grin. "I was terrible. I didn't really care, though, since school was my priority."

"Really?" My eyebrow rose. I couldn't imagine Kyler focused on school when I only ever saw him flirting or showing off on the field. "For some reason, I don't believe you."

"I'm serious!" His offense sounded fake, but he elaborated in an easy tone. "I'm really good at math. Science too. You might even call me a STEM genius." He leaned forward, gesturing me to come closer, before adding in a hushed tone, "In middle school, I was the fastest builder in our robotics club."

Now I really was impressed, but the Kyler he was describing seemed foreign to me. "Really? You made a robot?"

"Yeah," he said with a proud smile.

"Why'd you stop?"

His smile wavered a little. "I got busy," he replied. "Plus exercising really took my mind off things last year. Before I knew it, I was a first-stringer on the team, so I like to show off when I can."

I felt a guilty throbbing in my chest. I couldn't believe I hadn't thought about what he was going through last year. Of course he'd want to distract himself from the pain of losing his dad.

I tried to play along with his teasing. "I'm actually more into soccer players."

"What about gamers?"

That sounded like him. Now that I was starting to learn more about Kyler, gaming seemed more up his alley than football. Of course, leave it to him to be good at both. "Maybe." I smiled. "As long as they prioritize me."

"Don't worry about that, Brynn. You'll always be my priority."

—

WE WERE ON DESSERT BY THE TIME I REALIZED that all my earlier anxiety had completely faded away. Being with him was easy, which I found surprising. He was good at making the atmosphere relaxed with teasing remarks and sincere gestures.

We'd talked about everything from what made someone strong to what the worst vegetable was. The two of us argued and taunted each other for minutes on end. It wasn't that we disagreed, really, it was just that both of us had a strong need to explain the reasoning behind our thoughts.

It was fun.

"No way. That's not possible," Kyler said with a shake of his head. The corners of my lips lifted at the sight of his playful gesture. "You've never punched anyone before?"

I let a soft laugh escape my lips. "I've never needed to. People love me."

"Well, that I knew. It's hard not to."

I let the grin on my face widen. "What do you mean?"

"What do you think?" he asked smoothly, and I gave him a sideways look. His laugh barely rose above the banter of the rest of the restaurant when he leaned forward and continued, "I already told you, right? That I like you."

"And I already told you I'm not falling for that, but . . . thanks," I said. His intent gaze made me want to elaborate, so, after a pause, I continued, "You know, the whole thing with Ingrid and the school and . . ." And the nightmares. "It's kind of been a lot to deal with. But you've made going to school a lot more fun lately." I didn't have enough courage to look at him. "So, um, thanks."

ANN RAE

I began chasing around a raspberry with my fork. It was part of the cheesecake we'd ordered.

"You're going to thank me without looking at me?"

I lifted my head. Kyler's dark hair now drew shadows against his eyes, adding depth to his gaze as he smiled fondly at me. My chest clenched at the sight.

"It's the same for me," he said once his eyes drew mine in. "And it wasn't my intention to tease you as much as I do, but your reactions are so cute that I can't stop." He smirked like he knew how I'd react to that, too, so I glanced away and buried my cheek in my palm aggressively. Kyler let out a quiet laugh. "Like that."

"I'm going to get you back one day," I mumbled, sliding my eyes toward him. I kept my face turned away. "And you're going to blush harder than me."

"I'm looking forward to it."

I COULDN'T BELIEVE HOW DIFFERENT it felt on the ride home. A feeling of comfort washed over me as I sank into the passenger seat and caught a peek at Kyler. "That was really good," I said.

"Should we go again?" Kyler asked, tossing me a quick glance before focusing on the road.

I laughed. "Maybe."

We settled into an easy silence, and I realized that it'd been a long time since I'd felt this relaxed. At home I was alone, which meant I was always a little wary and on my toes. It wasn't any better at school, and probably even worse, since that's where everything had happened. It was exhausting feeling so anxious all the time, but having Kyler right next to me seemed to put me at ease.

"What are you thinking about?" he finally asked. The volume of his voice was low, but it struck me more in the dark.

"Oh." I started. I wasn't about to admit that I felt comfort in being by his side.

I wracked my brain for something to say before I remembered my earlier concern about Adalia and realized he might be a good person to ask. Talking to Liam and Adalia was great and all, but I didn't want to make them more worried than they needed to be. Especially when I was still unsure.

"Have you heard anything about Ingrid?" I asked.

His tone was surprised. "Ingrid? I've heard a few things. Are you asking about anything specific?"

I'm sure he knew about the incident. The whole school did, but I wasn't asking about that. "Have you heard anything about her since . . . well, you know. Like, have you noticed people talking about what happened to her? Or what was going on with her family around the time she . . . passed away?"

Kyler's expression grew confused. "Maybe. I haven't really been paying attention. Why? What's wrong?"

I inhaled. "I'm sure you probably know this already, but I was the one who found her on the bleachers. I haven't been able to stop thinking about it, and . . . I don't know. I know it wasn't an accident. I've been trying to listen for anything about her."

When I looked at him, his eyebrows were scrunched together. I was almost touched by how hard he was trying to remember. Finally, he said, sounding a bit unsure, "I've heard rumors about something illegal going on."

"Really?" I sat up in my seat.

Kyler seemed hesitant to respond. "I didn't think much of it, but if it's true, I don't think you should get involved, Brynn."

I shot him a glare. "I'm already involved. How can I not be?"

Kyler pursed his lips before continuing. "What if something happens to you? If they were fine with killing someone, then . . ." He didn't need to finish for me to know what he meant.

Of course, I'd had that thought a few times. If I got too close to the murderer, or the truth, maybe I'd be the next person to go. That'd been enough to put me off for a while, but now Adalia was possibly at risk, and I wasn't going to let anything happen to her.

Then again, maybe the risk was just in my head.

"I . . . I know. It's just that . . ." I trailed off as I realized that we were pulling up to my house. Kyler put the car in park and turned toward me. "I have to look into it. Adalia . . ." I hesitated.

"Adalia?" Kyler repeated, his eyes intent on me.

"I don't know. I might just be worried for no reason, but I've heard that Ingrid wasn't getting along with her parents. Adalia mentioned that she and her dad got into a huge argument about money, and it reminded me of that."

I felt guilty telling Kyler about Adalia's personal problems, but I didn't know who else to go to. Sure, I could tell Baylor, but he couldn't do anything. He didn't even live in this city anymore. I just needed to know if I was being paranoid or not.

I sighed and continued in a resigned voice. "I wish I knew why Ingrid was fighting with them. If it wasn't about money, then it could just be a coincidence, but . . ." My eyes pleaded with Kyler's. "What if it was? What if she went through something similar to Adalia?"

Kyler didn't reply right away, and I began to think maybe this was a line I shouldn't have crossed. Maybe it was something he didn't want to hear about, especially when things between us were always playful.

"I get it," Kyler finally said. "You want to protect her."

I nodded.

His touch was gentle as he reached for my hand. "But you're important too. Remember what we talked about in class? Don't endanger yourself to help others, Brynn."

"I won't." I shook my head. "I'm not trying to get myself killed."

Kyler gave a light chuckle, but he didn't look up as he focused on my hand, running his thumb over my knuckles and tracing the outline of my fingers. In the dark of his car, with just the moon reflecting off him, he seemed different.

"What are you going to do then?" he asked, meeting my eyes.

"I don't know. I was going to try and find out more about her. Listen to what people are saying. Get clues. I don't really have a solid plan," I admitted.

"I'll help you," he said.

"What?" I must've sounded more surprised than I thought because Kyler let out a laugh.

"I said I'll help you," he repeated. "I'm popular, you know. People tell me things, and now that I know you're interested, I'll try listening to them."

"You don't have to do that . . ." I trailed off, but my chest filled with warmth. I hadn't understood how alone I'd felt in the whole thing, but having Kyler declare his support affected me in ways I couldn't describe.

I felt like I could do anything. Take on anyone.

Even a murderer.

"I want to." He brought my hand up to his lips and brushed a kiss against the inside of my palm. "If you're okay with it." I was thankful for the dark. I didn't want him seeing how red my cheeks could get because of him. "I'm okay with it," I whispered.

"Good." He smiled. "If I hear anything, I'll write it down on a note and put it in our locker." His eyes flashed with excitement as if he were a kid learning a new game. "Deal?" My lips turned up. "Deal."

AFTER THAT VERY EVENTFUL DATE, I was tired. Kyler had walked me to the door like the gentleman I didn't know he was, and now I was plopped over on my bed.

Yet, I still had one more thing to do.

"How was it?" Adalia immediately asked, sparing the greetings one would normally get after dialing her best friend. I paused, letting the anticipation build up before my tongue flicked over my lips and I answered indifferently.

"It was okay."

"Really? I waited all night for 'it was okay'?" She scoffed on the other side of the cell phone as I set it down and put her on speaker. I pulled out my ponytail and watched as my hair formed a mane around my face. "You can do better than that."

"You expect so much out of me," I mumbled. "What do you want to know?"

"Details, Brynn! I want to know details! Where did he take you? Did he flirt? What happened?" Adalia asked in a frenzy, her high voice a bit lower with the echoing of the phone. I started brushing my hair.

"Well," I began, "it was a fancy place. Uh, the sushi restaurant near my house—"

"Oh my God, no way! The one with all the bottles in the window?" She practically squealed. I heard her hands clap together before she continued an octave higher. "That's, like, an anniversary level restaurant, and Kyler Fellan took you there for a casual date? He's totally trying to impress you. What else happened?"

My head flashed with the memory of his smile, and I found myself doing the same.

"Nothing," I said finally. "I mean, it was nice . . . really nice. He's different than I thought. He came to the door to pick me up and . . . I don't know. He looked really good." After a pause, I asked, "Should I pay him back?"

"No!" she shouted, her voice heavily contrasting the rest of the silence in the house. It was almost midnight, and I wondered how her dad felt about her yelping this late. "You should pay for the next date instead. You're an independent woman, but you also deserve to be treated."

My back flopped onto the blankets of my bed, the fluffiness bouncing me back up. "I guess you're right. What if there is no second date, though? How can you tell?"

"If he's flirting with you tomorrow, that probably means a second date." She giggled, obviously excited at the idea of romance. "I can't believe you're finally getting a boyfriend."

"Okay, okay," I said. "I think you might be getting a little ahead of yourself. But I'll admit I liked it. Just don't tell anyone, okay?"

"What? Tell them that you like Kyler or that you're getting a boyfriend?"

"Neither! Don't tell them anything!" I laughed, bundling my face farther into the softness of my comforter. "I'm going to sleep now."

"Okay! Me too. Get some beauty sleep," she chimed. "Good night."

"You too. Good night."

Then the line went dead, and the house was filled with sudden silence. I pulled up my laptop and turned on some music to offset the quiet. I didn't feel so alone with the music, and lately, I'd been sleeping with my old night-light.

I hadn't told anyone about that last part.

CHAPTER SEVEN

TALKING TO KYLER had revitalized my motivation. I'd always been alert when it came to Ingrid, but the past couple days had been different—I was hearing her name everywhere. People around the school whispered about her in the bathroom, the hallways, even by the drinking fountains during breaks. Everything was there for the taking; it was just a matter of being aware.

As I stepped out of my fourth-period classroom, I could hear it again. Ingrid. Her name dropped from the lips of a few girls I'd never noticed before as they huddled against the lockers in the hallway. Luckily, there was a vending machine near them, so I headed that way with slow steps and stopped in front of the glass.

"It's weird, right?" one of the girls said. I could only see the back of her head from where I stood, but I didn't want to make it obvious that I was listening by turning in their direction. "Ingrid said her parents cut off her allowance."

My blood turned cold. So the reason was because of money.

"But why? I thought her family was rich."

A shorter girl piped up, her voice just above a whisper. "They are. That's why she was so upset when they stopped. Maybe they got into a fight, and they wanted to punish her or something."

The first girl shook her head. "No, I don't think so. Ingrid said she didn't know why, which is why she was so mad about it."

"I wish we could ask her," the shorter girl said. There was a long pause before her voice came out soft, almost shaking. "I just want to talk to her again."

I tried not to throw looks of sympathy their way. I hadn't known Ingrid, especially not in the way they did, but her absence wasn't lost on anyone. That wasn't my priority, anyway. The fact that Ingrid's parents were now linked to some sort of lack of money made me think that Adalia's situation really wasn't just a coincidence and I wasn't acting overly paranoid. Her safety might really be at risk.

As they continued talking, I was almost tempted to go up and ask for more details, but I decided against it. I didn't want to involve more people than necessary, especially not when there was a killer on the loose. I'd just have to settle for listening like a fly on the wall.

"Are you almost done?"

An unfamiliar voice sent me spinning around in alarm. A boy stood there with a somewhat annoyed expression as he gestured to the vending machine. "It can't be that hard to choose a drink."

"Oh sorry," I said and stepped out of his way.

He gave me a confused frown as I backed away but didn't seem to think much more of it as he started pressing the buttons for a soda.

—

I DIDN'T HEAR ANYTHING ELSE OF NOTE THAT DAY, but what I'd gathered was still enough to feel satisfied. Satisfied but sorry, as hearing people talk about missing their friend was heartbreaking. I'd been doing my best to compartmentalize— solving the mystery of her death would be easier if I didn't focus on the personal aspects of it—but sometimes the tragedy of it all would catch up to me.

I tried not to get lost in thought as I made my way toward the locker room just after the last bell rang. My steps were slow, as I knew Kyler didn't take the notes until after practice was over.

But as I turned the corner into the locker room, echoes of deep voices and laughter surprised me. The boys' side was loud with chatter, which was unusual considering the time. I dug out the notes from my backpack; I'd written them during my office aide shift in fifth period. After the incident with Ingrid, I didn't have to do much there anymore. I'm sure they felt bad for keeping me past school hours, which shouldn't have been allowed anyway, but the fact that I'd witnessed a death because of them was enough of an excuse to say no to paperwork.

After putting in the combo of the lock, I swung the door open. My brows furrowed in confusion as a shirtless boy walked past, followed by another one with a jersey thrown loosely over his torso. Kyler's door was hanging open and giving me a direct view into the changing room, which, admittedly, I'd never seen before.

The top half of a familiar hoodie suddenly crinkled into view. "Brynn?" Kyler's quiet voice sounded surprised. Then his head turned as he realized I'd seen everything behind him, and he frantically closed the door on his side.

His quick reaction made me hold in a laugh. It wasn't like him to leave the door open like that, and the way he'd turned flustered was cute enough to bring a smile to my face as I dropped the notes in the locker and closed my door softly.

Just as I picked up the strap of my backpack and was about to head out, a faint click caught my attention. The door on the other side closed again, and when I peeked in, I noticed my notes were gone. A different sticky note was stuck onto the surface, and I plucked it off.

Even I can get jealous if you're
watching other guys change.

I blinked. Then I reread it until my face was pink and I was internally screaming. My hands fumbled for my phone as I quickly texted him.

I wasn't watching them!
YOU were the one who left the door open.

Just after I sent it, deep laughter chimed on the other side of the locker wall. I knew he was just messing with me, but I'd take it if my reactions let me hear a laugh as melodic as his.

I'D ALWAYS WELCOMED SATURDAYS with open arms, but that was even more true now that Baylor was a part of them. He always arrived at our house in the morning, and since I was in a good mood due to my encounters with Kyler over the past week, I decided to wake up and greet him before noon for once.

The sound of our front door opening propelled me out of bed, and I met Baylor downstairs.

"Hey," I said with a smile.

"You're up early," he mused. His face lit up with a smile as he scrambled my dark hair with his hand. "Usually I don't see you for a few hours."

"I thought I'd surprise you."

"Consider me surprised," he said. "Since you're awake, do you want to get some food?"

"Okay," I said. That idea was one of his best ones. "I'm starving."

He nodded to the door and put his stuff down. "I'll drive."

We ended up at a family-owned breakfast restaurant just a few minutes away. They served breakfast food all day, but they also had some really good lunch items like their grilled cheese sandwiches and salads.

The large room was decorated with simple decor and leather booths. It wasn't too busy for a Saturday morning, so I figured the regulars were still asleep or hungover from a wild Friday night.

My family had been coming to this restaurant for a long time. Our parents were friends with the owner, and their son, Baylor's best friend, Matt, had worked there for as long as I could remember. It was always fun coming to visit him at work, and he could get away with messing around since it was his family's restaurant.

Baylor and I sat across from each other at the booth, though Matt had squeezed his way in next to my older brother. They were the same age and had been close since they were babies. "So, what do you want to eat?" Matt asked from his seat. He was a tall guy with long limbs, unruly red hair, and an even wilder smile. He was as freckled as Baylor was tanned.

"I thought you were supposed to take orders standing up?" I asked, letting a small smile spread against my lips. "This isn't very professional."

Matt brought his hand to his chest in mock hurt. "This is what's called special treatment. Customers always want to interact with the merchandise." He gave a pleased grin.

Baylor swung his arm around Matt's shoulders and shook his head. "I think the merchandise is spoiled."

"How dare you." Matt gasped and slid out of his seat. "Just for that, I'm going to bring you the worst meal on the menu."

"This restaurant isn't capable of making something bad," I retorted.

Matt threw me a wink.

"But I am."

Then he disappeared into the kitchen, and I laughed. "You miss him, don't you?" I asked my brother.

"Yeah," Baylor said as he rested his cheek in his palm. "That stupid redhead makes my day. I wish he'd just finish his gap year and join me at school already." He sighed, and then his light eyes flickered up to mine. "Speaking of friends, have you made any new ones?"

His grin was teasing.

"As a matter of fact, I have."

"Really?" He sounded a lot more surprised than I'd expected him to, and I almost rolled my eyes. "Who?"

"They actually played football when you were a senior, so you might remember them," I started, but Baylor put his hand up.

"Your new friends are football players?" He shook his head, and the blond hair that'd been gelled up moved with him. "They're the worst."

"You're a football player. So is Liam."

Baylor paused like this was his first time hearing of such a thing. "All right, fine. I'll let it slide, but only because this town has an obsession with football that other sane towns don't. I guess I won't hold it against them." He crossed his arms. "So, what are their names? You said I might know them?"

"Um, well . . ." Now that I actually had to say it out loud, especially to my older brother, I was getting shy. In a mousy voice, I continued, "You know Kyler? Kyler Fellan?"

Baylor sat back in the booth as if pondering. "Kyler Fellan? Maybe. I don't really remember a lot of the freshmen."
"He said he wasn't very good yet, so maybe that's why. He's got brown hair, blue eyes, tall . . ." Attractive. So attractive I had a hard time tearing my eyes away from him. "Ring a bell?"

"Hmm . . . I think so. He was cute," Baylor said with a lingering smile. "A pretty boy who always showed up even though he didn't want to be there. I think I liked him."

"You did?" I almost sighed in relief. It would be a lot easier hanging out with Kyler if my brother didn't want to kill him. "Great. And the second one is Sterling. Sterling—"

"Reyes," Baylor finished for me. When I looked back up, his eyebrows were knit together, and he leaned forward, his hands clasped tightly. "That family is bad news, Brynn."

"What?" I couldn't believe my ears. Sterling was the embodiment of picture-perfect. He held doors open, he tried to include everyone—he wouldn't hurt a fly. "Are you sure you're thinking of the right person? Black hair, tan—"

"I know who you're talking about." Baylor looked quickly around the restaurant before lowering his voice. "His older brother was a mess. He had to leave town a couple years ago, and no one's heard from him since."

I'd never heard about that before. I didn't even know he had an older brother, much less one who had skipped town. "But Sterling might not be like his brother," I defended. "He's always been nice at school."

Baylor turned his head away. "I don't know, Brynn. Something about him was off when we played football together."

I frowned. Baylor wasn't the type of person to make up something like that. Sure, he was protective and didn't necessarily love it when I hung around guys, but his demeanor now made me worried.

"I'm back," Matt said suddenly. I glanced up at him as he placed two plates on the table. One was a steak omelet that Baylor always ordered, and the other was a skillet. A bit of my anxiety dissolved at the smell while Matt looked between the two of us.

"What are you two whispering about?" Matt asked as he slid into my booth. "Did something interesting happen?"

I pulled the plate toward me as Baylor took a bite of his omelet. Once he'd finished, he asked Matt, "Do you remember Sterling Reyes? A freshman when we were seniors?"

Matt's red eyebrows scrunched. "Sterling? I don't think so.

Why?" He grinned my way. "Did Brynn get a boyfriend?"

"*No*," Baylor and I said at the same time. I'd started coughing at the implication, but Baylor's eyes were fuming.

Matt's eyes widened before he put his hands up defensively. "Okay, okay, sheesh. I was just kidding."

I thought it was a good sign that Matt didn't remember Sterling—it meant he wasn't off enough to be on everyone's radar, just Baylor's. However, I trusted Baylor's intuition. He was studying criminal law, and he could tell when things were strange.

I hoped that he was just being biased against Sterling because of his older brother and not because Sterling was actually someone worth worrying about.

"Well," I said after eating a few more bites of my skillet, "I think Sterling's fine. If he does anything weird, I'll let you know."

"Just be careful," Baylor cautioned. "It's bad enough that our parents aren't here, but remember I'm only a few hours away if you need me."

Matt didn't seem to know what was going on, but he added, "And I'm only a few minutes away if you need me."

Baylor frowned. "Are you trying to one-up me?"

Matt feigned innocence. "Whatever could you mean? I'm just trying to be a reliable friend for Brynn."

My lips wavered into a small laugh. "Thanks, guys," I said. "I'll keep that in mind."

ONCE THE WEEKEND WAS OVER, I watched as my two best friends joked around next to me in the school hallway. Adalia yanked Liam's backpack handle backward as he tried to escape with her phone. Their laughter was contagious, and Liam threw the phone toward me. "Go long, Brynn!" he shouted.

Panic overtook me, and I just barely managed to catch her phone in the middle of the hall. I was as shocked as they were that I'd managed to keep it from shattering on the floor.

"Are you serious, Li?" Adalia yelled. "What if she dropped it! You could've broken my phone!"

"But she caught it! I had faith in her."

I shook my head. "How are you guys so energetic every day?" I was grateful for their energy, though, considering I didn't have much.

We entered the cafeteria and found our usual round table. After sitting in our normal spots, I couldn't help my gaze as it settled on Adalia. I studied her face, doing the best I could to identify her state. Was she doing okay? Maybe she was fine. It was hard to tell.

"What's wrong?" Adalia asked. The air around her was no longer playful as she caught me staring.

"Oh." I blinked. I didn't realize I'd started biting my nails, and Adalia gave me a small grin.

"Are you worried about me?"

"Of course," I said, tugging my hand down. "Is everything all right with your dad now? Did you guys talk?"

The light in her eyes seemed to go out as she focused on the table. "Kind of. It's not as awkward anymore, but . . ."

Liam's thick brows knit together. "What?"

"I just don't trust him. I feel like if I look away for a second, all our money is gonna go down the drain," she said, rubbing her temples. She sounded exasperated. "My uncle was talking about a possible job for me. Maybe I should look into it."

"A job?" Liam perked up. "Where?"

"That pizza place we go to sometimes. You know, the one with the retro theme?"

Liam's eyes shone. "I love the pizza there!"

Adalia's concerned expression morphed into something soft as she laughed. "I know."

"That could be fun," I said. "We can visit you at work."

"Yeah!" Adalia now sounded as excited as Liam. "Maybe it's the right move after all."

Before we got further along in the topic, two familiar figures started approaching our table. "Hey," Sterling said, his lips forming a soft smile as he looked at us. Kyler stood next to him, his eyes locking with mine immediately.

"What are you guys talking about?" Sterling asked as he sat down at our table. It'd become a common occurrence to eat with them lately, which I kind of liked. But I also felt an uneasiness after what Baylor had said.

Kyler's sudden touch brought me back to the moment; his hand slid down the small of my back as he sat next to me, and I felt my stomach jump. He did it so naturally that I almost felt envious—I wished I knew how to touch him without getting caught up in my head.

"I'm thinking about getting a job," Adalia said. "At that pizza place."

"Pizza place?" Sterling asked as he took a bite from his lunch. It looked like some kind of pineapple chicken dish he'd warmed up in the microwave, and I almost wanted to ask him to switch.

My PB&J probably wasn't a fair bargain.

"The one with the bright red couches," Liam elaborated.

Kyler's eyes flashed. "That place has the best breadsticks." And they really did, but it was kind of adorable that Kyler, in all his "I'm so cool" glory, got excited over breadsticks.

Sterling nodded as if he, too, approved of their food. My eyes began following every move he made, but nothing seemed unnatural. His body was relaxed, looking completely at ease as he brought his fork up to his mouth. No shifting eyes or scheming grins. He was just a boy eating his lunch in a cafeteria—completely harmless.

Baylor had gotten into my head, but I couldn't find anything off about Sterling. I kept my gaze on him a few moments longer before a deep voice pulled me out of my trance.

"Brynn," Kyler said, his lips near my ear. I shuddered at the sensation before turning in his direction and blinking.

"Yeah?"

"It's bad manners to stare at another guy in front of me, you know," he whispered. I swore I could make out a pout on his lips, and I tried to resist laughing. My initial impression of Kyler had been the cool playboy type, but now that I'd gotten to know him better, I realized he really was just a teenage boy with a cute side.

The other three were now talking among themselves, so I let my hand fall on top of his and grinned. "Are you jealous?"

His eyebrow rose, but the smirk he threw my way seemed challenging. Kyler laced our fingers together, and it almost felt scandalous holding hands under the table.

After our date, I'd felt a lot closer to him. It was different now that we had a secret together, and I found myself looking forward to the moments I got to talk to him or even catch a glimpse of his face.

That was probably a bad sign.

"So what if I am?" he asked. We were talking quietly, and the low timbre of his voice made me hang on to every word.

"Don't be," I said airily. "He's not my type." Then I brought my free hand to my chin and added, "Unless he secretly plays soccer."

Kyler laughed at that. "I don't think he does."

"Then you have nothing to worry about."

Kyler's blue eyes were sincere as he gave my hand a squeeze. "Good."

IT'D BEEN A COUPLE DAYS SINCE KYLER had caught me staring at Sterling, and nothing crazy had happened since then.

I'd gotten into the habit of checking my locker before going home every day. It was nice because there usually weren't many people in the room, which meant I got enough privacy to gather any notes or write them in secret.

I turned in to the locker room and heard a rustling noise from the other side. It got louder as I approached my own locker door, and when I started to work on the lock, I heard the noise stop.

I pulled the small door toward me. "Hello?"

"Brynn," Kyler's voice replied. I couldn't see his face, but I saw his hand lingering over a fresh note he'd put inside. "Hey. I was going to leave you a note, but this works better."

"What's up?"

"Listen, I have an idea," he said, crouching down just a bit. I lowered myself enough to meet his eyes. "I've heard stuff around school that makes me think something weird is going on. I think you're right."

"Wait, really?"

"Yeah . . ." he said. He didn't sound as excited as I was about being right, which was fair. "I don't know much yet, but . . . I think there might be people from school involved in all this. It just seems weird that we're getting so much information just from listening and talking to other people here."

Before I could respond, he added, "So I was thinking . . . it might be better if we kept our distance. Just so no one suspects us of trying to get information about Ingrid. If you're right, then things might really be dangerous, and I don't want—"

My words came out hurt. "Keep our distance?"

"Only at school," Kyler said quickly. "If we're both asking about Ingrid, and people know we're together, it'll be really obvious that we're trying to figure something out. It'll be easier to avoid that if we keep things low key."

What he was saying made sense, but I wanted to protest. My brain agreed, but my heart didn't. I wanted to be with him at school. I knew if we kept our distance here, we'd barely see each other anymore.

"Brynn?" he asked softly.

"Oh," I said in a daze. I was grateful he was putting our safety first, but I'd gotten so used to being around him at school. It made me sad to think about not seeing him as much or not being able to talk to him even when he was near. However, I knew his concerns were valid, and I had to agree, although reluctantly. "You're right."

"Hey," he continued, his expression serious as he looked at me. I almost didn't want to meet his eyes, although I knew my stubbornness was unnecessary. He wasn't doing anything wrong, and I shouldn't have been upset, but I was. "It's just at school. I still want to see you. We can meet at my house."

That got my attention. "Your house?"

"Yeah." He grinned. "My house. You can see my vacuum and everything."

"I guess that works. We can meet up at my house, too, since no one's home."

Kyler smirked. "That sounds kind of scandalous, Brynn."

"Maybe it is," I replied, matching his smile. Before he could get ahead of himself, I added, "Just kidding. You're going to keep leaving notes, though, right?"

He nodded. "Yeah. You too."

"Okay," I said.

"I don't have practice tomorrow," Kyler said, his face barely illuminated by his phone as he scrolled through his schedule. When he glanced up, I almost stared. "Are you free?"

"Yes." I didn't need to check any schedule. The only people I hung out with were Adalia and Liam, and we didn't have anything planned.

"Great." Kyler's smile was crooked. "I'll see you then."

THE NEXT DAY WAS A BLUR OF MIXED FEELINGS. Since Kyler and I had decided to stop talking at school, the easiest way to explain that was by "breaking up." I didn't love that idea, but there was no better alternative, so we'd been doing our best to circulate the rumor. I at least got to be the one to break up with Kyler, so I guessed that was a plus.

When I stepped out of class, ears ringing from listening to a long lecture, I felt my body collide with another one. I looked up wide eyed as I sputtered out an apology. "I'm so sorry."

Staring down at me were two guys. "You're good," the one I'd bumped into said. He looked at me for a second too long before a light seemed to turn on in his eyes. "Wait, you're Kyler's ex, right?"

So the rumors were doing their job.

"Yeah," I mumbled. The two guys both gave me sympathetic looks before the one farther away from me spoke up.
"Sorry, dude. It'll get better," he said, his eyebrows drawn up. I was actually kind of touched because although we hadn't really broken up, we weren't talking as much. Maybe I needed some consoling, even if it was in the form of two random guys.

"Thanks," I said. They both gave me nods before continuing on their way, which happened to also be the direction I was headed in. As I trailed behind them to my next class, I couldn't help but overhear their conversation.

"I don't think so, dude," the one I'd bumped into said. He was a little taller. "Life insurance doesn't work like that. Besides, what kind of high schooler has life insurance, anyway?"
"Maybe she did! Maybe she knew she was going to die, so she got it," the other one protested. "I heard she had a chronic illness too. So, you know, maybe she wanted to end with a bang and leave her family with some cash."

"You're crazy," his friend said. "Her family was rich, anyway. She wouldn't need to do that."

"Hmmm," the other one hummed as they turned a corner I didn't take. Their voices faded away as I continued to my destination, and I couldn't help but imagine what other rumors were circulating through the school. How many of them were true, and how many weren't? Although that rumor wasn't one of the bad ones, it was still ridiculous. Then again, the whole situation was ridiculous, or rather, tragic. I shook my head as I entered a class full of chatter and tried to ignore the extra looks I got since Kyler and I had decided to "end things."

I guessed I'd have to get used to it now.

CHAPTER EIGHT

KYLER'S HOUSE WAS ABOUT WHAT I'D EXPECTED after our date. He'd said his mom made enough money to keep them afloat, but I thought that was an understatement. The house was huge, and we sat in a wide-open living room where a window that stretched at least fifteen feet high illuminated the space. A faux fireplace divided this room and another one, but the open plan let you see everything: a sparkling marble kitchen, the railings that lined the second-floor balcony overlooking where I sat, and a giant TV that seemed like part of the wall. The TV hung over a shelf that had framed pictures of Kyler and his parents. There were a lot of pictures with his dad and a couple of just Kyler. One in particular made me smile—a younger version of Kyler, his brown hair tousled and his grin as proud as I'd ever seen, sat in a chair next to a laptop screen that faced the camera. I couldn't recognize the game, but I could see the bright *First Place* lit up on the screen and the small trophy he held in his hand. The light in his blue eyes shone bright, and I figured I'd ask him about it one day just to see if I could see that expression in person.

I sat on the white leather couch, my hands in my lap and my backpack by my feet, while Kyler sauntered in and placed a tray on the coffee table in front of me. It had two glasses of lemonade, a bowl of tortilla chips, and some guacamole.

I blinked.

I thought I'd felt out of my element at the restaurant, but being with Kyler in his own house made my nerves skyrocket. This was a completely different league.

Kyler fell into the space next to me, and I wished I could seem as relaxed as he did. He sat up and rested his forearms on his knees. "You're not allergic to avocados, right?"

"No, um . . . I like them." I groaned inside my head. *I like them*? I'd gotten used to hanging with Kyler, but suddenly it was like our first date. I didn't know what to say or how to act, and I wished I'd stop getting intimidated by things like big houses and fancy restaurants.

It wasn't like I was completely out of my element. I mean, our house was pretty nice too; we were upper middle class, as my mom would say, so I wasn't a stranger to fancy dinners once in a while. I liked to watch HGTV with my mom, and this house reminded me of the houses I'd seen on there. I was in awe of the house, sure, but also of the fact that this was Kyler's home, where he lived and had grown up, and it seemed to have more of an effect on me than I'd expected.

Kyler smiled as he scooped some guac onto a chip. "Me too." Then he reached down and pulled out his own backpack. "I brought all the notes, like you said, so should we go over them?"

I nodded a little too eagerly. I was grateful to have something to do besides sit awkwardly and crane my neck around the room. "Yes," I said, unzipping my backpack and shuffling through folders. I found the notes he'd written and displayed them on the table.

He spread out the ones he'd collected as well. It was silly, but it made me happy knowing that he carried around my hand-written notes.

There weren't more than ten notes altogether, but it was enough to work with. "So what made you think something weird is going on?" I turned to Kyler. His narrow face rested in his palm as he frowned at the pile.

"Here," he said, reaching forward and drawing a sticky note toward us. "It's like you said. It'd be a coincidence if Ingrid was having problems with her parents because of random stuff, but it wasn't."

"They were arguing over money," I confirmed. I'd looked over the notes already, but talking everything through made it easier to comprehend. "I heard some girls talking about it in the hallway."

He nodded and then picked out two more notes. He placed them next to each other. "They took away her allowance first. That's what those girls said, right?"

"Yeah. Ingrid was mad because she didn't know why her allowance suddenly stopped."

"Some of the guys I talked to said that her parents even asked her for money."

I frowned. "I wish I knew Ingrid better. Maybe this would all make more sense. Did you ever talk to her before?"

"No," he said, a sadness tinging his voice. "I never thought to."

"Yeah," I whispered. "Me neither. But we're going to figure it out. There was another note, the one talking about her dad."

"Right." Kyler snapped out of it, and his eyes scanned the table. "This one. Ingrid's dad had a bad reputation at work because he asked to borrow money from his colleagues."

"Was it always like that?" I asked. "Or was it just before the incident happened?" The answer would be important, especially because of Adalia.

"I think . . . it was recent. The people I got the info from said that their parents were talking about it because they were worried. Apparently he changed. It was like he'd become desperate overnight."

I brought my hand up to my temple. "That's not a good sign."

Kyler looked at me in confusion. "Why?"

"Adalia," I said. "Her dad started acting like that out of nowhere too. I mean, he's never been the responsible type, but he's never been this reckless either. That's why she was more concerned than usual." I sighed before picking up a tortilla chip and dipping it into the guac.

"Do you think I should tell her?" I asked after biting the chip in half. "I don't want to worry her, but I don't like this. I don't like how similar she and Ingrid are sounding right now."

Kyler brought his attention back to the notes. "Would you want to know?"

"Yes," I blurted. I didn't even need to think about it.

Kyler gave a weak smile. "Then there's your answer. I wish you'd hesitated a little more, though."

"I think it's always better to know the truth."

"Always?" Kyler asked before reclining on the couch. "'Ignorance is bliss' is a real saying, you know."

"Well, I don't use it," I replied defiantly. Then I took a sip of lemonade, and Kyler's eyes were on me. I quickly glanced away. "What?"

"I just think you're cute," Kyler mused.

"Yeah, right," I mumbled into my cup. I tried not to feel shy, to give him the satisfaction, but I couldn't help it.

"You never believe me." His voice was softer than usual, defeated, and it plucked a string in my heart. Maybe I shouldn't have been so quick to dismiss him.

When I put the cup down, I glanced at him. "Sorry. I just . . . it's so easy for you."

"What is?"

"Saying things like that. Calling me cute. Touching me." I tried not to sound bitter, but it made me upset. It was embarrassing getting excited over all these small things when they didn't mean anything to him.

Kyler's brows furrowed. "It's easy because I mean it." He must have realized this was important to me because he elaborated. "I just say what I think in the moment and do what I want to do. When I think you're acting cute, I'll say it. And if I want to touch you," he started, his hand coming to cup my cheek, "I will. Unless you tell me not to."

My brain went into overload as I stared at him. "So you really think I'm cute."

"Yeah," he said. His lips quivered, and I could tell he was holding back a laugh. "I do."

"Fine. I'll believe you if you tell me why."

His eyes widened. "You want reasons?" When I nodded, he hummed. "Okay. Just now," he started, leaning closer to me, "you stood your ground."

"What? About always wanting to know the truth?"

"Yeah," he said. "And about Ingrid. And a lot of things. I like that you go for what you think is right, even if other people don't agree. And I think it's really cute when you get mad or stubborn because of it."

I bit the inside of my cheek to keep from smiling. I hadn't realized that about myself, and the fact that Kyler paid enough attention to me to know that felt good.

His fingers brushed against my cheek as they moved to circle a fallen strand of dark hair. I wore my hair in a ponytail, the same style I'd worn on our date. "And I think it's cute when you put your hair up," he said. "It's cute when you look away because you're shy. And it's cute when you bury your face in your hands, and when you laugh at my jokes, or laugh in general. I think it's cute when you focus so hard you look mad. It's cute when you—"

I put my hand over his mouth, my cheeks finally starting to burn. "Okay, okay," I said in defeat. "I get it. I believe you."

His eyes lit up, and I pulled away.

"Really?" Kyler asked.

My face felt so hot I didn't want to look at him as I nodded.

"You don't need more examples?" Mischief laced his voice. It sounded nearer now.

"No," I mumbled.

There was a sound of rustling, and when I finally looked his way, he swept his lips against my cheek and kissed me.

"I'm glad," he said, sounding satisfied. Then his phone started to ring, and I barely caught a glimpse of *Mom* lighting up the screen. "Oh, one second," he said as he accepted the call and brought the phone up to his ear. "Hello?"

I could just make out the high voice on the other end, but I couldn't understand what she was saying. Kyler noticed me looking and grinned. "Yeah, I'm home. I'm with my . . . friend."

The fact that he hesitated before saying friend made my heart thump just a little, and Kyler's face seemed to heat up. "Yeah, that one. Sure." His expression took on surprise. "Right now? I mean, yeah, I can ask her." When he turned toward me, I tilted my head. He covered the speaker with his hand. "Do you want to stay for dinner?"

"Dinner?"

"Yeah, my mom is picking up some food on her way home, and she said she wants to meet you if you're not busy. It's not anything fancy, just takeout. But no pressure. Sorry for springing it on you."

The offer was tempting. Of course, I was already nervous just sitting in his house, and I didn't think I was prepared to actually meet his mom. However, I wanted to. It was Kyler's life, and I didn't know if I was overstepping, but I wanted to learn everything and anything I could about him, about how he saw the world and what kind of parents raised him. I wanted to see a different side of him—how would he act around his family? Would he make expressions I'd never seen before?

"I'm not doing anything, so if you're okay with it," I said shyly.

"I'm okay with it," he said with a smile.

"Then I'll stay," I said.

"Great," he replied before turning back to the phone. "She said she'll eat with us."

—

THE SOUND OF THE GARAGE DOOR opening propelled Kyler up from the couch, and he was quickly at the door into the garage from the house, opening it just a crack. "Do you need help?" he asked.

"No, it's okay!" I heard from inside the garage. The sound of her voice reminded me of how real everything was—this was actually happening. I was about to meet Kyler's mom. He held the door open as a woman stepped in, her arms wrapped around a takeout bag. She had a similar facial structure as Kyler, with a narrow face and straight nose. Her hair was lighter than his, and her eyes were a darker shade of blue. She gave a beaming smile when our eyes locked. "Hi! You must be Kyler's friend," she said as I frantically stood up. "You can call me Leana."

"Yeah, hi, my name is Brynn," I said, not sure how natural that sounded. I felt my weight shift on my feet as I leaned in her direction. "Do you need help with that?"

Her laugh was an airy sound, fitting for the attractive woman she was. Her hair was up in a clip, and the blazer she wore seemed modern. Leana was already walking toward the kitchen island when she called back, "Despite my age, I am capable of bringing in some food."

I felt my face go red as I followed her to the island. Kyler was by my side, and I couldn't tell if my words were fumbling or not. "I'm sorry, that's not what I—"

Another chime of laughter cut me off. "I'm just teasing. Come here," Leana said. She began unpacking the containers of food, and I watched, trying to identify what was mine.

Kyler was next to me when he spoke. "Stop messing with her,

Mom," he said with a roll of his eyes. He placed his hand against mine in a reassuring manner, and I felt relief and butterflies at the same time.

"She's so cute, though," she replied with upturned lips. She tossed me a quick wink before bringing our attention back to the food. "Now, help me unload these tacos onto some plates."

It only took a few minutes until the taco-filled plates were set onto a large glass table. We each had a cup of water, which Leana insisted on adding lemon slices to. I sat at one side of the table, Kyler across from me, and his mom at the head.

I looked down at my food; I hadn't realized how hungry I'd been until the sight of chicken tacos with mango salsa made my stomach rumble. Once I realized Kyler and his mom had already taken bites of their food, I decided to follow their lead and was shocked at how good it tasted.

I was already a few more bites in when Kyler's mom spoke. "So, how's school lately? Have things calmed down?"

It'd been a while since I'd had a parent ask about my school day during dinner. I found myself missing my parents a little more as I thought of an answer. I couldn't say things had calmed down, per se. Rather, the school was full of hungry teenagers who didn't care about what was right or wrong—just what was interesting. "There's always something going on," I replied with a small chuckle. I took a few more bites of my food as Kyler nodded.

"They always find something to talk about because they're bored," he added.

"High school can be rough," she answered, her head shaking. "It gets better when you have people you like, though. I promise."

I knew she was right. Pictures of Adalia and Liam popped into my head, their smiles and jokes making things more fun. Kyler's image formed in my mind, too, and I almost forgot I could just look ahead of me and see him in person. When I did, our eyes caught, and before I realized he was already looking at me, he had hastily turned his head away.

"This food is good, Mom," Kyler said quickly, and I tried to contain my smile. I still couldn't get over how cute he'd act sometimes—it always took me by surprise.

"You think so?" she asked happily, looking back down at her own taco. She had one left. "This place just opened, so I thought I'd try it out. What do you think, Brynn?"

"It's really good," I answered. I was almost embarrassed that I didn't have any food left on my plate. "I'm glad it's not too spicy."

"You don't like spicy food?" Kyler asked from across the table.

I shook my head. "No, I can't handle it."

"I don't really like it either," Leana said with a small smile. "But Kyler's dad loved spicy food, so I bet that's where he gets it from."

"Yeah," he said. His lips broke out into a wide grin. "His taste was better than yours."

"His cooking was too," she answered with a sigh. "Do you cook, Brynn?"

I glanced at Kyler curiously. Maybe he'd mentioned it to her, but his face didn't give anything away as he threw me an easy smile. "I like cooking, but I'm still practicing."

"I'm sure you're better than you think," Kyler said.

—

AFTER WE'D FINISHED EATING, we talked more about the basic things, like what my parents did, how many siblings I had, which subjects I liked the most, etc. I had to admit that both Kyler and his mom had a knack for making people feel at ease. Once we started talking, I almost forgot how nervous I'd been at the thought of meeting Leana. I was excited to talk to her more in the future, and even that thought made me somewhat embarrassed.

I handed a cup to his mom as she began to wash it in the sink. Kyler was outside throwing away the trash, so we were by ourselves. "Thanks so much for dinner," I said over running water.

"Of course!" she answered, tossing a kind look from beside me. "I'm so glad I was able to meet you. Kyler has mentioned you a few times, so I was getting curious."

"Really?" The surprise in my tone must have been more obvious than I thought because Leana gave out a laugh.

"Yes, really," she said with a lingering smile.

"What . . . um, what did he say?" I asked, handing her a plate this time.

"Unfortunately, I can't give away his secrets like that," she answered playfully. She began scrubbing the plate, her eyes focused on the task, but her lips still curved. "But even if he hadn't told me anything, I can still say this . . ."

I looked at her expectantly, and she continued. "He's been a lot happier these past few weeks. I assume you know about my husband's passing, and, well . . . it was rough. I know Kyler's been doing his best for me since then, but it feels like he's not trying as hard around you. He smiles more, you know? He's just laughing because he feels like it." Then she turned to face me, her eyes shining against tan skin. "So thank you. I know it's cliché of me to say this as his mom, but I'm glad he let me meet you."

I didn't have to feel my face to know it was warm. It was warm in the best way—sure, I was shy, but I was also ecstatic that he was feeling as happy as I was. The fact that even his mom had noticed and had taken the time to tell me made me want to run to him right then and there.

"I'm glad I got to meet you too," I said before the door leading into the garage opened. The two of us turned our heads in the direction of the sound, and Kyler emerged, his hand running through his hair as he glanced out the wide window.

"It's getting pretty dark," he said, and I followed his gaze. He was right. It was just past seven, and I was almost upset the sun couldn't wait.

"You're right," I said. "I should probably go."

Kyler's mom gave a nod. "Of course. It was nice to meet you," she said, pulling off her wet gloves. Then she pulled me into a hug, and my eyes went wide at the sudden contact. It took me a moment to relax into it, and when she pulled away, I noticed the smile lines around her mouth. "Get home safe, all right?"

"Thank you," I replied, my lips upturned.

"I'll walk you to your car," Kyler said as he walked across the living room. He nodded toward the front door. "C'mon."
I followed him out the door after saying good-bye to his mom one more time. The fall air bit at my nose as I walked beside him, watching the wind rustle through his brown hair. When we were by my Jeep, I spoke up. "Your mom is really nice."

Kyler grinned. "You liked her?"

"Of course I did," I said. My voice got quieter as I found the ground with my eyes. "I hope she liked me."

Sudden warmth wrapped around my hand, and then Kyler's fingers were interlaced with mine. "Who wouldn't like you, Brynn?"

I tightened my grip as I looked up at him. The smile he wore was dazed as he looked down at me, his half-lidded eyes entrancing mine. I couldn't help but step closer to him, my spare hand lightly gripping his sleeve. "It was really nice," I said, "learning more about you."

When Kyler gave me a questioning look, I added, "I mean, like, seeing your pictures and talking to your mom . . . I don't know."

Kyler smiled. "So you were looking at the pictures, huh?"

"Only the one of you with a trophy," I said playfully.

His eyes widened as his cheeks flushed. Then the sound of his laughter, so free and almost innocent, echoed against the dark sky. "The worst one for you to look at."

Kyler's happiness was contagious. "You looked cute," I said.

"And what about now?" he asked, his voice laced with mischief. "Am I still cute?"

"Hmm . . ." Then a smile broke out on my lips. "Maybe a little."

He laughed again. It was such a nice sound that I didn't want to say anything to get in the way, but it eventually faded away, replaced by the hoot of an owl. Both our heads shot up, trying to find the source of the sound, before Kyler spoke up. "You should go now," he said, his head just barely looking around. "I don't want you getting home too late, especially when you're alone."

"You're right," I said, a bit disappointed. I knew I should go home, but I'd been having such a good time with him that I wanted to stay longer. "Thanks for dinner."

"Come over whenever you don't want to eat by yourself," Kyler said. He swung our arms in unison, and when he looked back at me, his eyes shone. "I mean it."

"Okay," I said. There was something about the atmosphere, about the cold air and the night sky, the fact that we were alone together, and the experience of just having met his mother that made me want to be a little bolder than usual. I bounced up on my toes, my hand steadying myself against his shoulder, and planted a kiss on his cheek. "Good night, Kyler."

I didn't give him much time to respond before I jumped into the seat of my Jeep and took off.

I might've imagined it, but when I looked back in my side mirror, his hand was against his cheek, right where I had kissed him.

FRIDAY'S CLASSES HAD GONE BY QUICKLY. It was Friday night, which meant Adalia, Liam, and I were finally free from immediate homework and wanted to go somewhere to celebrate. Luckily for us, Adalia had accepted her uncle's job offer, so now we had a new spot to hang out: the pizzeria. The environment was warm, with the scent of cheese and bread floating through the air, tickling our noses and skin. We were in a red booth with a shiny red lacquered table, and since the theme was retro, this place was always packed with high schoolers.

"God, you look like a mess," Liam said, poking me in the arm with a breadstick.

He was probably right. I'd been trying to figure out how to bring up the money issue with Adalia, but I'd been failing miserably.

I tried to hide my discontent at being jabbed at with a greasy piece of bread before Adalia clicked her tongue, aiming her gaze at a carefree-looking Liam. He relaxed farther into the booth as he shrugged and took a bite of the breadstick. "What?"

"You're still going to eat that?" she asked, repulsion obvious in her expression. "Gross."

"Hey, at least I'm not wasting it!" he said before turning his head so he could better see the door to the kitchen. "How long does it take to make these, anyway?"

"I don't know," she said, reaching out to take one from the middle of the table. "I haven't started working yet. He said I can start training next week." With a smile, she added, "I think it'll be fun."

"I can't believe they're actually going to hire you," I said, earning an exaggerated glare from her.

"I visited the other day to meet some of the employees. They're really nice," she said before taking a large bite. Liam watched her with a small grin on his face, but he didn't say anything as she looked back at us. "The guy who's going to train me is—"

"Wait, guy?" Liam interrupted, the smirk leaving his lips immediately. I had to cover my mouth with my hand to keep from letting a small laugh escape, but he didn't seem to notice as his eyes squinted just a fraction. "I thought you said you were going to work with a girl."

"Well, yeah, but she had to switch her shift," she said. "Why?"

He hesitated before sighing. He ran his hand through his hair as he leaned against the table. "Nah, it's nothing. So what about this guy?"

My heart went out to my two best friends. I knew that Liam had never stopped liking her, but due to their close friendship, he never crossed that line. Adalia was sharp, observant, so she either saw how Liam felt and ignored it or chose to lock those thoughts away and remain oblivious.

I knew she valued him a lot, though—maybe even enough to convince herself that she really couldn't see how his eyes lit up when he looked at her.

She continued a little slower, with a crease in her brow. "He just seemed really anxious. I don't know. It makes me anxious too. A lot of things do lately."

Maybe this was the time to tell her. I took a deep breath, "Adalia," I said softly. My two friends must have sensed that something was off because their attention was fully on me now. "I found something out, and I thought it would only be fair to let you know."

"What is it?" she asked nervously.

"You know how you told me that Ingrid was fighting with her parents?" Adalia nodded. "Well, I found out why. Apparently, they'd been arguing about money. Her parents cut off her allowance and even asked her for money."

There was silence in the air aside from the background chatter of other patrons who were completely oblivious to our state of crisis. My two best friends were smart enough to make the connection between what was happening to Adalia and what had happened to Ingrid.

"I don't know if it's anything to be worried about," I added. "But it did remind me of your situation, and I just wanted to let you know. Maybe we should be careful. It could be a coincidence, but . . ."

Adalia let out a breath. "Thanks, Brynn. For telling me." She paused. "I don't know what to do."

Liam's expression was hard. "Nothing's going to happen to you, Ad." He placed his hand over hers. It covered it completely. "Maybe you should try talking to your dad, get more information from him."

Adalia looked defeated as she gave a slight nod. "Yeah. I think that's a good idea. I will."

"Ad—" I started.

"Adalia! Thank God you're here," a deeper voice interrupted from the side of our table, belonging to a boy who looked a little older than us. He had deep pink cheeks, darting eyes, and fumbling hands that clutched a clipboard. He wore a name tag that read *Ethan*, and I couldn't help but notice how Liam's arms crossed as he leaned back, his frown evident as he looked over the boy who'd come running up to our table.

"Ethan? What's wrong?" she asked, her voice edging into concern.

His hand rubbed the back of his neck as he looked at the floor. "Uh, well, can I, uh, talk to you over there?" Ethan nodded his head at a different area of the restaurant.

"Yeah, sure," she said, sliding out from her seat next to Liam as she followed the other boy away.

"Do you think he's the one training her?" I asked.

"Maybe." Liam glanced in their direction. "I hope so. Maybe he'll do all the worrying for her." His expression seemed down. "This sucks, Brynn. All of this. I hate watching both of you go through everything and not being able to help."

Affection swelled in my chest. "You are helping, though. You're definitely helping Ad. You make us forget that things suck, so maybe keep doing that?" I offered a grin.

He copied it. "Yeah? Okay, I will. I'm great at using humor as a coping mechanism."

I snorted, which made Liam's eyes go wide. Then we were both laughing.

Adalia came back at the same time, her feet bouncing as she arrived at the table. She slammed her hands flat on the surface, which made both of us look up in surprise. Her eyes dashed from Liam to me as she put on a stern expression.

"Are you guys busy tonight?" she asked.

Liam and I exchanged glances.

"I'm not," I said.

"I have to babysit my brothers," Liam grumbled. "Why? What's wrong?"

Adalia brought her hand up to her forehead. "Apparently, two people called in sick tonight, so Ethan asked if I could start training early. My uncle said it was okay, but we still need a little more help, so I was wondering if one of you could stay back with me?"

Liam looked like he was cursing his brothers. "I would, but . . ." He sighed. "Sorry."

"I can help, I guess," I said. "I don't have any experience, though. I might make it worse."

"It's okay! We'll find you something really easy to do. And don't worry about it, Li." Adalia's earlier worry was replaced with a new sense of excitement as she went back on her toes.

"AM I WEARING THIS RIGHT?" I mumbled, my fingers failing as I tried to wrap the apron around my waist. I let out a small curse as I turned in a circle, attempting to see the string dangling behind me better. Adalia's laughter came into earshot as I scowled at her. "Hey, I'm doing this for you."

"I know," she said with a chuckle. She took a step closer and finished tying the red apron on me, and, with a sigh of relief, I thanked her.

"What are friends for if not to tie fabrics?" she said.

"I don't think I've ever heard that one before," I commented, but she shrugged, a smile still lingering on her face.

"So, let's go over what you're doing," she said as we sat down on the small circular stools in front of the counter. "You don't have to cook anything. You also don't have to take any orders. You're just going to bring out the food, and then we'll take care of the rest, all right?"

It seemed easy enough, but I found myself wishing Liam were there too. He was always better at multitasking and dealing with people, and I was worried I was going to make a fool out of myself.

"Okay, got it," I said, nervousness fluttering in my stomach as I looked around the room. There were six or seven tables filled with people, but thankfully, they'd already been served.

Adalia reached out to pat my head. "I can tell you're nervous." She gave me a wink. "Don't worry about it. Seriously. Just think of it as a quick way to make some money."

I nodded in agreement just as the boy named Ethan walked up to us. He looked a little more composed now that the issue had been resolved, but that didn't keep him from continuing to bounce on his toes.

"Um, you guys ready? Our shift starts now," he said. Adalia gave an eager nod as she pulled me off the stool, but I could tell that she was a little nervous too. Having this much work to do while still in training couldn't have been easy, but Adalia was the type who liked a challenge. "Brynn, right?" He looked at me. "You just stand behind this counter, and we'll tell you which pizzas go to which tables."

"All right," I said, trying to calm the butterflies in my stomach.

Sadly, they weren't very obedient.

But as time went by, I started getting the hang of balancing the pizzas on the trays and carrying out boxes for those who'd ordered them. It really wasn't that hard, especially in comparison to watching Adalia wait tables. I watched in awe as she briskly moved from table to table with a smile on her face. She wrote orders quickly, sticking them on the back kitchen counter before getting drinks out to everyone. She didn't look like she was training at all.

As it started to get a little later, she walked past me, giving me a thumbs-up as I set down a pizza at one of the tables. When the bell on the door rang, both of us looked up.

The deep laughter of five teenage boys added to the sounds of the restaurant as they made their way inside. They seemed familiar, and a moment later I realized they were from Westwood. The bell above the door rang once more, and I held my breath as I watched Kyler walk in and slouch against the wall, watching his friends with uninterested eyes as they debated where to sit.

Adalia's head shot back in my direction, giving me a wide-eyed look that only a best friend could give.

"Kyler, hurry up! I'm starving," Jayden called out as he approached a table with some of the others. He caught my eye and broke out into a smile. "Brynn!"

Then he realized his mistake as he glanced back unsurely at Kyler, who was still propped against the wall by the door. He knew that we'd broken up, but apparently it had slipped his mind as he'd waved to me. I tried to resist laughing. Jayden was like a golden retriever, and I knew he couldn't help being friendly.

I gave him a small wave, and he looked relieved.

I didn't wave at Kyler, but the look on his face was enough for me to know that he saw me. I didn't personally know any of the other guys in that group; Sterling wasn't with them.

In a flash, Adalia was at their table with her notepad, asking what they wanted to drink. I let my chin rest in my palm as I tried to find other places to look, like at the two people in the corner on a date or the group of older men all getting riled up over a baseball game on the TV.

A couple of minutes passed before I got tired of hearing an older man with a baseball cap shout, "Knock 'em dead!" every five seconds. The man next to him hit him in the face with a slice of pizza, yelling at the same volume, "Shut up!" Ethan had to rush over and ask them to quiet down, though he was shaking the entire time.

I decided to take a bathroom break. It looked like no one needed my help anyway, and maybe it wouldn't be a bad idea to make sure my hair wasn't a complete mess in front of Kyler.

After I'd freshened up, I took a step outside the bathroom door. Kyler was near the supply closet, and just as I was about to say his name, his eyes met mine and he quickly brought a finger up to his lips. My voice died out as he nodded toward the frosted-glass closet door and disappeared behind it.

I glanced around the hall quickly before sneaking after him. I peeked up as Kyler reached behind me and closed the door.

"What are you doing?" I asked as playfully as I could. The closet was tiny and dark, and we were nearly chest to chest; the idea of being so close to him made my heart drum. He had held my fingers and brushed my face before, but having hardly any space between our bodies was different.

"Kidnapping you," he said, looking down with a flash in his eyes. I could feel how his voice resonated against our bodies.

"You're not supposed to kidnap the waitstaff." My voice wavered with a laugh, and he grinned.

"I couldn't help it."

"What if someone sees us?" I whispered, glancing back behind us. The door was blurred, which meant you could make out figures but no details through the window. "We're broken up, remember?"

Kyler didn't seem concerned.

His fingers trailed under my chin before gently tugging my

head in his direction. Then my face was in his palm as he gazed down at me so softly I could melt.

"Your beauty mark." He spoke quietly. His thumb brushed against the bottom corner of my eye. "I forgot to mention that in my list of cute things about you."

It felt surreal. Muddied voices floated outside, but I couldn't make out a single word. It was dark around us, and I might have been imagining it, but his breathing sounded as shallow as mine. Every word he said, every move he made, felt amplified by our proximity to each other; I inched forward, wanting to get as close as I possibly could.

"Kyler," I said, just to hear his name from my lips.

He pressed our foreheads together. "I didn't know you worked here too."

"I don't," I said with a small smile. "I'm just helping Ad today. There was an issue with the staff." My voice sounded far away, and something about the atmosphere, about the way he spoke and looked at me, made me feel brave enough to be as affectionate as I wanted to be.

"Well, I'm happy." His lashes seemed fuller when he gazed down; they swept above his cheekbones, and I couldn't help but touch him. His eyes widened in surprise, but he didn't move as my fingers slid down his cheek. "I was going to text you, but seeing you in person is better."

"Text me? About what?"

"Do you like parties?" His hand started moving down from my face now. The action was smooth as he skimmed my arm and rested his hand on my waist.

"Sometimes," I said coyly, my fingers hooking on the loops of his pants. "Why?"

His breath hitched in his throat before he spoke. "Sterling is having a last-minute one tomorrow night. It's for the football team, but we can bring anyone." His eyes reflected my image. "You should go with Liam."

I had a vague recollection of Liam bringing it up and Adalia seeming excited for it, but knowing Kyler would also be there sealed the deal of my attendance.

But I didn't tell Kyler that.

"You know," I started, "you're the one who suggested we keep our distance." I almost laughed at that, considering the position we were in. "I think it'd send mixed signals if people saw us talking at a party."

"We can hide," he suggested. When I raised an eyebrow at him, he laughed, and I could feel it. "I know that house inside out. It'll be fine, I promise. I just . . ." He tightened his grip around my waist. "I want to be with you. I think it'll be fun."

"Okay," I agreed. "I'll go."

"Yeah?" His tone was excited.

My laugh came out airily. "Yeah."

CHAPTER NINE

"I'M HONESTLY SURPRISED," I told Adalia as I spun around in her chair. Adalia pressed against my shoulders before muttering, "Stay still!" once again. I hated doing my hair, and I knew Adalia hated doing my hair too. Especially because I could never stay still when she played with it.

"Surprised about what?" she asked, though it was hard to make out what she was saying with bobby pins clenched between her teeth.

I glanced at our reflection in the mirror. Her long hair was parted to the side as the rest fell in a natural curve, looking full and beautiful. My dark hair contrasted hers dramatically, with strands that fell straight. She was giving me the half-up, half-down look I always loved on her.

"I'm surprised that I'm actually looking forward to tonight. It'll be nice to relax a little, you know?"

Her twinkling eyes met mine in the mirror before she laughed lightly and picked out a pin. "I know what you mean." Then her smile turned mischievous. "You're excited to see a certain someone, aren't you?"

"Oh shut up." I swatted her arm gently but couldn't conceal my own grin. Liam and Adalia knew about the whole "pretending to break up" thing with Kyler. It was weird; we'd never actually been dating in the first place, but sometimes it had felt like we were. I didn't really know what we were, but I knew that I was too deep now to deny I had feelings for him.

Adalia dabbed a little more makeup on my eyes and cheeks before giving me an approving thumbs-up. "You look great!" She glanced at the clock. "And we're going to be late. We better go."

We both clambered up and grabbed our jackets from her bed. The two of us raced down the stairs in her house and burst out the front door before I took a hold of her arm and stopped. "Hang on, you're going to mess up your hair if you run that fast."

"My hair is indestructible, thank you very much." But she took a deep breath and started walking to the car at a slower pace. "Sorry, I'm just really excited. Plus, I don't want to make Liam wait too long. I think he's already there."

"He can wait a couple minutes," I said with a reassuring look as I opened the door and slid into the driver's seat. "Besides, you know he's the type of guy who can talk to anyone."

"Yeah. Yeah, I do," she said with a lingering grin. Then she closed her door, and I hit the gas.

The ride to Sterling's house didn't take too long, but my nerves started acting out once we pulled up and noticed the number of cars parked on the street. I was dreading being surrounded by people who smelled of sweat and alcohol. It was fun sometimes, but it'd been a while, and my stomach was starting to churn in anticipation.

As we stepped out of the car, we could hear the music pumping from his house, despite being almost a block away. The air was cool as we walked toward his house, but I decided to keep my jacket off, knowing how hot it would be with everyone around.

And when we opened the front door, it was. Hot and loud. I could feel the beat of the song thumping through the floor as people I recognized from hallways danced on each other, laughing, making eyes, doing whatever they wanted. I almost winced at the thought of how this house would get turned upside down come morning.

Adalia tugged my arm with an encouraging smile as she pulled me through the crowd, the two of us muttering apologies as we bumped into strangers, but when our eyes finally landed on Liam, a wave of relief washed over me.

He brought the two of us into a tight hug, and, after releasing us, he leaned down. "Follow me," he shouted, though I could still barely hear him. "I know a place that's a little quieter. And less crowded."

We nodded along quickly and let him drag us away from the sounds and smells until we reached the kitchen, where the air became breathable and, surprisingly enough, didn't have many people.

But leaning against the counter, in a half conversation with some people he didn't seem too interested in, stood Kyler. His eyes drifted across the room until that familiar gaze settled on me, and I forgot how to breathe.

Kyler grinned like he knew.

"Do you guys want anything?" Liam asked, swinging his arms

around our shoulders. Adalia brought her hand up to his, causing Liam and I to share a surprised look. He glanced down at
where their hands connected and gave a giddy smile. It seemed
like he'd forgotten I was watching, though, because he suddenly
shot his head up in my direction and gave an awkward cough.

"Is there any light stuff? I'm driving me and Brynn back,"
Adalia responded, completely oblivious to the effect she'd had
on our best friend. She began pulling the two of us toward the
fridge before she finally noticed Kyler and paused with a coy
smile. "I know you love taking shots of vodka with cranberry
juice, Brynn."

She said it a little too loudly, and I knew she was letting Kyler
know.

He gave her a quick smile before ending his conversation.
Then he picked up a small bottle of vodka, the large bottle of
cranberry juice, and his own drink. No one seemed to mind as
he slipped away, and I tried my best not to make it obvious I was
watching him.

"Hey, guys," a voice said from behind us. I turned in surprise
to see Sterling, his usually tanned face now flushed a glowing
red. He gave us a silly grin.

Liam copied it. "Hey, man!" They did that hand greeting
all guys in high school do. Adalia smiled, too, although she
refrained from any hand gestures.

"I'm glad you guys made it," Sterling said. He held a cup in his
hand as he leaned against the kitchen island. "I didn't expect so
many people to show up."

"You're just too popular," Adalia joked. I let out a small laugh
and nodded.

"She's right," I said.

"I guess it has its perks," Sterling said. He gestured toward the scattered bottles of alcohol with a nod. "I only bought one of those."

Liam whistled. "Maybe I should host some parties."

Adalia actually laughed at that. "I'm sure your little brothers would love that. No one parties harder than a six-year-old."

"I'm still upset I had to babysit them last night. I wish I could've helped you instead," he grumbled, his dark eyes finding the floor.

"What happened last night?" Sterling asked as he took a sip of his drink. It reminded me of the drinks Kyler had taken, and I was beginning to wonder if he was ever going to text me where he'd gone.

"Work," Adalia sighed. "I had to start earlier than we thought."

"At the pizzeria?" he asked.

She nodded.

"How do you like it? My friends that work are always complaining about their shifts ending so late," he said.

"I like it so far. My shifts are supposed to end at seven, so it won't be too bad," Adalia said lightly.

"Should we go again?" I asked Liam.

"I never get tired of breadsticks," he replied.

Liam and Sterling began talking about their favorite places to get pizza, eventually making a ranked list of the best pizza toppings, before I got the long-awaited text.

First room to your left in the basement.

Goose bumps tingled up my arms in excitement. I knew it was nothing, but sneaking around the way we were made everything feel so much more fun. "I'm going to the bathroom," I said quickly. Adalia must've known what I was hinting at because she gave me one of her "looks."

"Do you need me to show you where it is?" Sterling asked, pushing himself up from the counter, but I shook my head almost frantically.

"It's okay! It can't be too hard to find. I'll be back," I said. Before Sterling could say anything else, I slipped out of the kitchen and sent a text to Adalia and Liam, telling them where I'd be. Then I searched the house for stairs.

The only difficult part about it was pushing past hordes of people, but the lights were on and the layout was simple, so I finally found the basement door, barely cracked open, and made my way down the stairs.

There were only a few people in the basement, lingering around an old couch and TV, but they didn't notice me as I eyed the left side of the room. Before I could scan the wall for doors, however, their conversation suddenly took a turn I was interested in.

Two guys and a girl stood around, all of them with a cup in their hands. One of the guy's faces was bright red, and the girl next to him watched as if concerned. "Dude, I told you guys already," he said, his words almost slurring, "she had a secret boyfriend. That's why she was on the bleachers."

"Really? Why would you think that?" the girl asked.

"Didn't you hear them talking about how someone said there was a guy there too? My bet is that they got into a fight, and he pushed her down the stairs or something." The mention of that night sent my mind back to the scene of her body—the scene when I'd found her, when she was just a fresh, limp corpse on the ground. Chills ran up my arms. I didn't want to get into my head, not tonight, and I decided to leave before I could hear more.

They were partly right, of course. But I didn't think it had been a secret boyfriend.

I shook away the thoughts as I looked for Kyler. The first room to my left had a closed wooden door. I prayed it was the right one as I timidly turned the handle and peeked inside.

"Kyler?" I whispered.

There he was, leaning against a high table in a small room. Wine bottles were stored in a geometric pattern off to the side, and the table he was leaning on looked like it'd been a bar at one point.

"Hey," he said. "Close the door."

"Right." The door behind me creaked shut, and I glanced around the room. It was mostly wooden with a dark floor, a tiny window at the very top of the wall, and a black counter. I made my way next to Kyler, suddenly feeling shy at the memory of how close we'd been yesterday.

My gaze tore away from his face and aimlessly ran down his torso, his arms, and to the cup he held in his large hands. Red liquid sloshed against the sides as an orange slice floated at the top.

He must've noticed me staring because he held up his drink. "Wanna try some?"

"What is it?" I asked.

"Jungle juice." He took a sip of it and shrugged. "They mixed a bunch of alcohol in it, but it's not bad. Here."

Kyler handed the cup to me, and I raised it to my lips uncertainly. The alcoholic tang covered my tongue, and only the slightly sweet taste of orange juice kept me from gagging.

Kyler's eyes brightened as he laughed before taking the cup back and setting it down. "Not your thing, huh?"

I wiped my hand against my mouth and made a sour face. "Not really. Maybe I'll just take a few shots and be done."

"So I heard." Kyler nodded behind me, and I turned to see the pink bottle he'd grabbed from upstairs. "I'll match you."

"Really?" I asked. "How much have you had already?"

"A little." He grinned. "I was waiting for you."

I couldn't help but feel touched.

He unwrapped two small plastic cups that were already in the room and poured in the clear liquid. I tried to keep from grimacing as I held it in my hand, but his encouraging smile gave me a tiny leap of courage. "Ready?"

I nodded. We clinked the cups together before tapping them down against the table, throwing our heads back, and downing them. Tears welled up at the strong taste, and my hands fumbled for the cranberry juice, trying to wash away that gross taste with something overwhelmingly sweet instead.

"Do you want some?" I asked, my head shaking as if it would effectively shake the taste away too.

"It's okay. That's all for you."

"Wooow," I teased. "He's too cool for a chaser."

"Of course I am." He gave me a wink.

We took a few more, and by the time I was done with my third shot, my cheeks were heating up. The sound of music from the living room was still loud and clear down here, and I figured the vents must've been helping. Every thump pounded along to my heart, and I almost started dancing.

"You know," I said, giving him a loose grin, "I really like this song."

"Yeah?" Kyler's eyes seemed to sparkle as he held my hand and swayed our arms to the beat. "I really like you."

I didn't respond right away. Kyler's features were too entrancing, and I had to take a moment to stare. I liked him too. He'd told me so many times that it was only fair to let him know.

Nerves rushed through my chest at the thought, and I decided to do it later. Maybe after another shot. Or two. My hands tightened around his, and Kyler's smile made me feel giddy, like I was a little kid again. "Really? You really do?" I asked. He spun me around, and I burst out laughing. No one was in here to watch us, and Kyler must have been feeling as light as I was.

I had a suspicion his tolerance was higher, though.

"I really, really do." He grinned, knowing it sounded as ridiculous as it did. My eyes trailed over his face and lingered on his upturned lips. They'd brushed against my hands so many times, but never anything else. I wondered what they'd feel like pushed against mine, if they'd feel soft or warm.

I tried to snap out of it.

"Okay, Kyler," I said quickly. Maybe a change of scenery would help. I tugged at his arm and prompted him to stand up. "It's too hot. Let's go outside."

He followed me as I tried to locate the back door, which probably took longer than it should have. We didn't run into

anyone on the way, and I had a small suspicion that maybe Kyler
had been leading me from behind, but I didn't want to admit it.

When I stepped outside, the cool air kissed my face, and I
blinked at the fairy lights hung against the wooden panels of the
patio. The music was quieter out here, and I figured the cold
weather kept most people from coming outside. A couple of
chairs were placed against the wall.

I liked having Kyler by my side. I wanted him to be there all
the time, but I didn't know how to tell him that. Maybe I was
getting ahead of myself, especially after drinking, but it didn't
stop me from taking quick peeks at him as many times as I
could.

"Do you want to sit?" Kyler asked while doing a bad job of
holding in a laugh. The moonlight lit up half his face, shadows
defining all those perfect lines and edges. His eyes shone even
brighter out here, and I couldn't control my gaze as it wandered
toward his lips. They parted again. "Brynn?"

My eyes shot back to his in a panic, and he tilted his head, letting his hand trace a strand of hair before tucking it behind my
ear. "Your cheeks are red," he said, his voice low, captivating.

"Because of you," I replied. Or maybe it was the alcohol. The
two combined were almost fatal.

"It's my fault?" His laughter was a sound I wanted on a record
player. "That's cute."

"You're cute," I said without thinking. I bounced on my heels. "I
don't really feel like sitting down. The world is moving too much."
And it was. Things would tilt if I walked, with one side of my body
feeling heavier than the other when I took a step. Luckily, we were
standing in place.

"It's moving?" Kyler's eyebrows scrunched together as he scanned the backyard. "Stay here," he said finally. "I'll find you some water."

He disappeared around the corner, and I leaned against the wall, watching bright stars peek from behind the silhouettes of branches and distant roofs. Then my eyes closed, trying to still the slight feeling of spinning as I wrapped my arms around each other. It didn't help.

Time seemed to go by slowly. My breathing was loud in my ears, as was the thump of my heart and the footsteps that approached.

"Brynn." His voice sounded so nice. My eyelids fluttered open to see Kyler's face close, and I smiled.

"You're back."

"I'm back," he said gently. He pulled out an unopened bottle of water and handed it to me. "You should drink some water. It'll make you feel better."

"Oh yeah." I twisted the cap off and let the water flow past my lips. I tipped it up too far, though, and extra water splashed back. I blinked in surprise before lowering the bottle and watching Kyler laugh.

His laugh died when he met my eyes.

I wasn't the type to stare, or maybe lately I was, but something about tonight made me feel like I could do anything I wanted to. Right now, all I wanted to do was look at him.

Kyler came closer, his eyelashes dark as his eyelids dropped just slightly. "Brynn," he whispered softly. His hand cupped my cheek, and I felt his thumb run against my bottom lip. "You spilled some water."

I ran my eyes down his face and toward his wrist until I couldn't see anything. With my eyes closed, I waited to see if he was feeling the same thing I was. The sounds of people were distant, but the sound of the night was loud. Even louder was Kyler's presence, right in front of me, as I felt him brush closer. My fingertips trailed his cheek.

My lips parted, and not even a second passed before his mouth was against mine. It was soft at first, but he pulled back, a wild look in his eyes. "Brynn." My name came out like a rumble. "Is this okay—"

I cut him off, and my lips collided with his. He steadied himself against me, his hands firm against my waist, my wrists locked around his neck. His lips were as soft as I'd imagined as he deepened the kiss and pulled my body against his. The coldness of the night didn't matter anymore. Not when he was so warm and so close.

This time, I pulled back, just to catch my breath. His eyes were half-lidded as they watched me, his chest rising fast, his hair unruly after I'd run my fingers through it.

"Kyler," I whispered, drawing him closer by the back of his neck. He followed along willingly until our foreheads touched. When he looked at me like that, so intently, with a face so flushed, it was almost hard for me to say what I wanted to. But I'd already made up my mind.

"I like you."

Surprise washed over his expression before his lips turned up. He brushed them against my mouth so gently you couldn't call it a kiss.

"I already knew that."

CHAPTER TEN

THE NEXT MORNING, I HAD A HANGOVER. Adalia and Liam seemed fine over FaceTime, while I had to continually turn the volume down to soften the tones of their voices against my pounding head.

"So, brunch?" Liam suggested.

It was a tradition we had to get brunch after a night of partying. It was supposed to help with hangovers or something—apparently eggs were good for that.

"Can we do dinner instead?" Adalia asked. She'd slept over last night but left early this morning to go get ready for her shift. "I have work today, so I don't get off until seven."

"I guess that can be arranged," Liam said with a grin. "Should we do it picnic style? What do you think, Brynn?"

I'd been half-buried in my blankets. It was too early for a conversation like this, but I mumbled a yes. "Picnic style sounds fine."

"You better set an alarm," Liam said with a tsk. "I know you're just going back to sleep once this call is over."

"Yeah, yeah." I yawned.

Adalia fumbled with her fingers in her own frame before finally coughing. "Um, I know this isn't the right time to bring it up, but . . ."

Liam's head perked up. "What's up?"

Her sigh echoed through my phone. "I checked our bank account again, and it was worse. Like, a lot worse." Her brows furrowed together. "I confronted my dad, but you know what he said? He yelled at me and said it was for my sake."

Adalia's voice took on a hoarse edge. I hadn't heard her sound this angry in a long time. "I can't believe he's using his own daughter as an excuse to throw away money."

Liam must have had the same thought as me. "Ad . . ." he said unsurely.

She shook her head. "I just wanted to keep you guys updated." Then she gave a weak smile. "I need this picnic too. It'll be really fun."

Liam nodded vigorously. "Superfun."

"Superfun," I repeated.

FEELINGS OF UNEASE WERE AT AN ALL-TIME HIGH as Liam and I walked up the hill toward Lakeview Park that evening. The yellow moon reflected against the water, its shape deformed and blurry with the movement of the lake. Fallen leaves crunched under my boots as we headed a little farther from the road; it was too dark to tell what color they were.

"Is she almost here?" I asked Liam as we stretched out on the fuzzy blanket. Warmth engulfed my body as I snuggled farther into my hoodie and kept my beanie snug over my ears. My ears always got cold easily, and living in Colorado when it was this chilly made beanies a lifesaver. Crisp air swept against my red nose and cheeks, and I wished I'd brought a scarf too.

The actual lake was dimly lit, but the sidewalks that traced the hills were covered with streetlights. The park here was generally safe and, luckily, never too populated. It gave us enough privacy to complain about our issues and also drink a little without making fools out of ourselves.

We'd already brought the snacks and everything else. Champagne was snuck into three different Hydro Flasks, and we had a large jug of orange juice. The only thing missing now was Adalia, but her shift should've ended about fifteen minutes ago.

"I don't know. She's not texting me," Liam said, pulling out his phone for the fifteenth time. The screen illuminated his face as his eyes furrowed. "Maybe she had to close—"

His phone suddenly chimed, and we both glanced at it eagerly.

Ad is sharing her location with you.

"What the . . ." Liam trailed off, his eyes squinting as he held the screen closer. Then they popped wide open. "Wait."

He was quick when he pulled up maps. Her location was moving fast, and she wasn't near us or the pizzeria anymore.

"Where is that?" I asked with a quiver in my voice. I bundled the blanket up as quickly as I could while Liam rose to his feet and pulled out his keys.

"We have to go. We have to go right now," he said. His words were sharp and edged with worry. I ran after him, snack bags threatening to slip from my grasp, before sliding into the passenger seat and letting them all fall. The fear of losing her the way we had lost Ingrid made my hands shake. We weren't going to let anything happen to her. We couldn't.

The two of us were out of our parking spot and headed toward the main road in seconds.

"Keep updating her position," Liam commanded, and I gave a firm nod. After driving for another five minutes, her location came to a halt.

"Wait, Liam," I said. "It stopped. Let's speed up."

His foot pounded the gas, and we went way above the speed limit. When we finally reached our destination, we were surrounded by trees on a dirt road. There were no streetlights. Suddenly, I felt even more unsettled.

"What is that?" I leaned forward in my seat. My hands trembled from adrenaline mixed with fear. "An abandoned barn?"

Liam copied my action before pulling into the lot. "I think so." He glanced around. "I don't see her car. I don't see any cars, actually."

"Me neither," I whispered. We both got out of the car quietly, stepping on the ground as softly as we could. We were only about ten feet away from the barn, so we crouched low. I did my best to avoid any fallen twigs from the trees that surrounded the barn. Everything about it felt wrong: the standalone barn, the lack of streetlights or signs, and the fact that there were hardly any footprints in the ground. This place must not have been very popular.

We followed the outside wall before turning the corner and noticing a light shining through the window. "Someone's in there," I whispered.

Liam cursed. "There's no chance you've got a weapon on you, is there? We can't just go in there—"

"I have pepper spray." I lifted my keychain in front of him, holding the keys together so as not to make them clang. "Do you want it?"

"Are you okay with that?"

"Yeah."

Liam gingerly took it in his hand before we peeked through a small window. Inside was practically empty, although a few haystacks remained by the wall. I could make out the shape of two figures, both wearing masks, and Adalia tied to a chair.

Adalia had binds against her hands and feet and a blindfold over her eyes.

I could feel Liam tense up next to me in anger. He shot up to run in before I tugged him back down. "Wait!" I hissed. "Do you have a plan? Should we call the cops?"

"You call the cops," Liam said. "I'm going inside."

Before I could stop him, he pushed past me and opened the door. My shaking fingers dialed 911 as I watched through the window.

"Nine-one-one, what's your emergency?"

"Hi, um, my friend has been kidnapped. We followed her location to this abandoned barn, and she's tied up to a chair, and there are two guys with masks in there. My friend just went in with pepper spray."

"Where's the barn?"

"I—I don't know. It's past the main highway, like fifteen minutes north of Lakeview Park. Please hurry and send someone, I—"

"We're sending someone right now. Stay on the line."

The rest of what she said was a blur because now there was shouting, and I couldn't stand it any longer. I pushed past the doors and found my way behind Liam as he held out my pepper spray.

Clearly, one of them had already been attacked. The burning smell bit at my eyes and nose as I stepped in, coughing into my sleeve and trying to shield my face with my other arm. "Oh my God." I coughed again.

"Are you stupid?" the one who hadn't been sprayed yelled at his comrade, who was crumpled on the floor. His voice was distorted, and he wore a Halloween mask. "You didn't check to see if her phone was on?" He coughed too.

His figure was tall and lean, and his hair was clearly black. I didn't want to imagine what he looked like behind his mask, not when his tone was so cruel. The man kicked his sidekick in the stomach before turning on his heel and heading toward the back door. He wasn't running, but his long legs carried him quickly out of sight.

"Wait!" The smaller one scampered up, his hands gripping his stomach as he tried to stand. "Please!" His feet shuffled against the ground before he darted away, desperately trying to make his way out. He was swaying as he tried to run, and I knew he was partially blinded from the spray.

"Oh no, you don't," Liam yelled, ready to launch after them before Adalia began frantically shaking her head.

"No! Don't—don't leave, Li," she cried. Adalia trembled in her chair, unable to see anything, and I decided it was safe enough to go to her. I ran in her direction and pulled off the blindfold. Then I threw my arms around her neck.

"It's okay, Ad," I whispered through the sleeve on my nose. "It's me. I'm here."

Liam did a double take before taking a step in the direction they'd run to. He was fast, really fast, and the small one seemed to realize that he hadn't made enough headway to escape. He made it past the doors, out of sight, and just as Liam was about to follow, a rock came flying toward him.

There was a small cracking noise as it hit Liam on the side of the head, causing him to falter and take a step back. Liam brought his hand up to his head before snapping out of his initial shock and continuing after them.

The sound of an engine shook the barn just as Liam stepped out the back doors. "No!" he shouted, his voice louder as the sound of the car faded away. "No, no, no!"

A few moments passed before Liam trudged back inside, the side of his forehead leaking blood.

"They're gone."

As I leaned against Liam's car, with blue and red lights flashing against the trees, I felt an unwelcome sense of familiarity. Everything in me wanted to leave and get away from this situation. Memories that I'd dreamed about were starting to feel real again, but with one look at Adalia, trembling and small, I knew I had to stabilize myself. For her sake.

Police wandered around, some examining the chair, others ignoring the tire scrapes behind the back door.

Adalia wrapped herself in the blanket that I'd grabbed from

the park while Liam stood firmly by her side. They'd given him a bandage, although none of us thought that was too effective. We planned to stop by the hospital on the way home.

"So." A man in a uniform finally approached the three of us. "Unfortunately, we can't really do anything. You were only able to provide vague descriptions of the kidnappers, and the car tires are too common to match with any specific vehicle. There was also no license plate, so all we can say is try to stay inside at night."

"What? That's it?" Liam slammed his hand against the hood of his car. "You aren't going to do anything? We told you the height and what they were both wearing. Isn't that enough to start looking?"

"Look, without proper evidence, we can't—"

"Are you even trying to find them? Adalia got kidnapped! Do you not get that? If we didn't find her, she could've been . . ." He trailed off, his anger forming into worry as he glanced at Adalia. She kept her head down, but her fists remained tight around the blanket.

"It's unfortunate. We'll keep looking, but don't expect much. You all should go home." The police officer glanced at Liam's head wound and winced. "Maybe get that checked out too."

Liam stood up to protest some more, but I latched on to his arm. "Liam." I spoke softly. "Stop. This is how they are. This is what happened with Ingrid, and this is what's going to keep happening. We can't expect anything from them."

His eyes sharpened into a glare.

—

THAT NIGHT, WE FOUND REFUGE at my home. Baylor hadn't been able to come up this weekend, so it was just the three of us in the living room. Liam had been diagnosed with a concussion, and Adalia was upset but no longer shell-shocked from the incident.

"I hate them," Liam mumbled. His arms were crossed as he sank into the couch. "How can anyone be so useless?"

"We know they suck," Adalia said, placing her hand on his shoulder. "Brynn found that out at the beginning of the year."

"But . . . are you okay? I mean, what did your parents say?" I asked, holding a hot cup of tea to my chest. I'd made one for each of us, and even Liam, who hated tea, had finished most of his.

"They're mad. And grateful, you know, for you guys. I hope they don't start fighting again."

Liam gave her a look of sympathy.

"You were smart to send us your location like that," I commended.

"Thanks. Yeah, I was just in the parking lot of the pizzeria, and this guy came up and . . . ugh." She shook her head at the memory before her eye caught on something. "Brynn, your phone is ringing."

"What?" I glanced in the same direction to see my phone aglow with Baylor's profile picture and name displayed on the screen. Just as I reached out to decline the call, Adalia spoke.

"You should answer," she said.

I frowned. "Are you sure? Baylor can wait."

Adalia shook her head. "It's fine. He might get worried if you don't pick up."

She had a point.

I answered the phone and quickly walked into the kitchen, just a short distance away from where they sat. "Hello?" I asked.

"Brynn," he said, relief lacing his words. "I said I'd call you since I couldn't come up this weekend. How come you weren't answering?"

I blinked. "What do you mean? I answered just now."

"I've already called you three times."

Surprise took over as I checked my call history and realized he was right. I must not have noticed since we'd been in the hospital with Liam.

"Oh," I said hesitantly. "Sorry. I was . . . playing on the Switch with Ad and Liam." I didn't think it would be a good idea to tell him everything that was happening because I knew he'd tell me to stop. If I told him about Adalia, he'd probably figure out what I was up to.

Kyler and I had already come this far with deciphering Ingrid's murder, and I knew Baylor would do everything he could to make sure I was safe. Obviously, trying to find a killer wasn't the safest thing you could do.

Baylor was silent for a moment. "I thought Adalia didn't like playing on the Switch."

I glanced at Adalia sitting on the couch. Liam was talking to her and making her laugh as best he could, but I knew now wasn't the time for me to be on the phone with Baylor. I needed to be with them. "She wanted to get better," I said quickly. "Anyway, now you know I'm fine, so everything's good, right?"

I started bouncing on my toes, eager to end the call and get back to my friends. "What? I mean, yeah, but are you sure everything's okay—"

"Yeah, I'm sure! Good night, B," I said.

"Um, good night," he replied just a second before I ended the call. Then I was rushed of the kitchen and back into the living room.

Once I was back in my seat, the three of us continued debriefing, and a thought popped into my head.

"You know what's weird?" I said. I wanted to say something, but maybe it was too soon. Adalia gave me an intense look, and I knew she wouldn't want me to keep anything from her. "Well, that last guy, the tall one? The one who kicked the other guy?"

"Yeah?" Liam asked. Adalia looked confused, as she hadn't seen either of them with her blindfold on.

"He kind of reminded me of Sterling. I don't know. His hair and his build were similar. Obviously not his voice or the . . . way he kicked that guy, but . . ." I stopped, not sure if I sounded crazy or not. I might have been speculating because of what Baylor had told me: something about Sterling was off.

"You're right," Liam agreed, and relief washed over me. "He did kind of look like him. I was thinking the same thing."

"Yeah." I nodded. "But I'm not sure. I mean, we couldn't see his face or anything."

"It's enough to be cautious," Adalia stated. "We should keep our distance. Just in case."

The two of us agreed.

CHAPTER ELEVEN

School wasn't great the next day. Liam had a concussion, Adalia didn't even come, and I was feeling down about the whole situation. It was really scary thinking about what could have happened if Liam and I hadn't shown up at that barn when we did. It was a true stroke of luck that she'd been able to share her location with us.

The thought made me sick.

Liam looked like a zombie, trudging along the hallways, his eyes barely open, and I wondered how similar I looked.

"Do you think she's eating?" Liam asked as he walked me to class. He kept glancing at his phone, and I saw he'd been checking up on her all day. "Sometimes she forgets to eat when she's upset."

I'd been texting her, too, but I knew she felt more at ease when Liam did. Even if she denied it, he was special to her, just like she was to him.

"She told me she had yogurt," I answered. It was exhausting just to talk. We'd been up all night, and now school felt like a pointless thing to waste energy on.

"Yogurt," Liam repeated in a trance. His eyelids were drooping as we walked, and he almost drifted into some lockers before I pulled him back on track.

"Careful," I said. "You already have a concussion. You don't need another one."

He scratched the back of his head. "Right." Then his eye caught on something, and I followed his line of sight. "Hey, it's Kyler."

Kyler stood at the other end of the hall, a couple friends surrounding him. His hand gripped his backpack strap as he noticed me, and his dark eyebrows knit together when our eyes met. He stepped in my direction before pausing and thinking better of it.

I glanced at Liam. His usually bronze skin was paler now, with dark hues under his eyes. If Liam looked like that, I probably looked worse, and Kyler's reaction to seeing me only helped confirm that guess.

I took a deep sigh. My concealer was really letting me down these days.

"How's it going, by the way?" Liam asked, his voice low as he leaned toward me. "With . . ." He nodded at Kyler.

"It's going good," I said. I thought about the night of the party, but I was almost too exhausted to smile at the memory.

"And . . . have you guys learned any more about . . . you know," he asked, our steps mirroring each other. Last night, I'd come clean to him and Adalia about what Kyler and I were up to with the investigation. I'd kept it a secret, mostly because I didn't want them to worry about me or think I was getting obsessed, but I thought Adalia deserved to know after what she'd gone through.

Before that, they'd known Kyler and I were still hanging out in secret, but nothing else.

I shook my head. "We haven't talked since the party, so I'll let you know if anything comes up later."

Liam gave a tired nod. "Thanks."

AFTER CLASSES WERE OVER, I continued my daily habit of going to my gym locker to check for updates. I wasn't really in the mood to deal with solving crimes right now, but if it meant there was a chance to protect Adalia, I'd take it.

Upon opening the locker, however, only a single note greeted me. I plucked it from the surface and couldn't help the warm smile that spread against my lips.

Are you all right? Call me.

So I did.

An hour later, Kyler was at my house, and things felt like they'd be okay again. He took a step inside and closed the door behind him.

"Hey," he started. I clasped my arms around him before he took a step back, and he steadied his arms around me. The rhythmic beat of his chest rising and falling made me feel at ease, and I couldn't help but bury my face closer.

His movement was tender as he smoothed out my hair and patted my head.

We stayed like that for a while. I'd been exhausted all day, but I hadn't realized how tired I really was until I was with

Kyler; he made me feel safe, comfortable, and I nudged closer. After a few more minutes, I led him to the couch and pulled my knees toward my chest as I rested against the cushioned arm.

I explained everything that had happened the previous night, and Kyler listened, his eyes intent as he nodded along. "I knew something bad was going to happen," I muttered softly. "It's the first time I'm upset that I was right."

"I can't believe you guys went through that," he said, his voice low. It hinted at anger.

"Me neither. I'm just so glad that Li and I found her."

Kyler nodded.

I wanted to tell him our suspicions about Sterling, but I didn't know how he'd react. Would he be mad? Defensive? I didn't want to cross the line. As I peeked up at him, debating whether or not I should say it, he tilted his head.

"What's up?"

If it was somehow related to Sterling, he should know.

"We think . . . well, we're not sure, but . . ." I stumbled over my words as Kyler sat patiently, his hand finding my back. His fingers ran idly up and down my spine as I continued. "One of the guys who kidnapped Adalia looked kind of familiar."

Kyler's eyebrows rose. "Really?"

I gave a small nod. "We might be wrong, but . . . I don't know. He kind of looked like Sterling."

Kyler's hand froze, but he didn't look mad.

That was a good sign.

He didn't respond and instead stared at a spot on the couch for a while as his fingers started weaving through strands of my hair. I wondered what was going through his head. I couldn't even hope to guess.

"Kyler?" I asked quietly.

He looked back at me in a daze. "Oh. Sorry. I'm listening."

I gave a small smile. "Are you okay? It might not have been him."

"I'm fine," he said. Then his hand dropped, tightening around my waist, and his gaze became hard. "I'll protect you whether it's Sterling or not."

"You'll protect me?" I grinned, and Kyler came closer. His smile seemed playful, but the way he moved and the way he touched me so gently seemed at odds.

"I mean it, Brynn," he said in a low voice. Then he kissed my forehead and looked back down at my upturned face. "I won't let anything happen to you."

THE NEXT DAY AT SCHOOL FELT OFF. The morning had been rough; I'd been late, burned my breakfast, and hit a pothole. So it wasn't off to a great start. I thought at least seeing Kyler would cheer me up; although we couldn't talk to each other, he'd still send sneaky glances my way. It was fun, thrilling almost, when we made eye contact.

But today had no stolen glances, which I thought was weird.

Even when I initiated it or looked his way, he'd flash his eyes somewhere else, and I'd be left standing there completely confused and embarrassed.

That feeling stayed with me until I checked my locker during third period. There was usually a feeling of giddiness when I saw one of his notes waiting for me, but this one was different—my heart hammered in uneasiness because I knew it probably wasn't going to say something good. The note crinkled as I opened it.

Trust me.

I frowned. That wasn't much to go off of, and it didn't seem like Kyler was eager to elaborate, either, not when he couldn't even look me in the eye.

Although it was upsetting, I tried hard not to let it get to me in obvious ways. Adalia was back at school after her recovery day, and that was more important. She'd been trying so hard to act natural, like nothing had happened, and I wasn't going to let her efforts go to waste by acting down over a boy.

Even if it was a boy I really liked.

THE STADIUM LIGHTS WERE BLINDING.

It amazed me how football players became immune to the brightness, but I guessed it was essential for them. You couldn't play if you couldn't see. In this cold, though, I was more than glad I was just a spectator.

Adalia and I had decided to finally come to a football game to support Liam. However, I also wanted to try talking to Kyler.

I knew he'd told me to trust him, but that had been a week ago, and nothing had changed except for the fact that he was impossible to talk to. There were no new notes in my locker. And every time I texted him, it remained unread. I trusted him, but it was obvious he wasn't telling me something. Maybe it was him who didn't trust me.

To be honest, I was mad. Really mad.

I'd thought we were in this together, but the way he was acting made me think otherwise. I had to talk to him tonight.

Adalia bounced on her toes next to me. She wasn't talking as much as she normally did, but that was probably because she was trying to keep her teeth from chattering. Since neither of us was that invested in the actual game, we snuck out to the concession stand beside the bleachers for some hot chocolate.

There was a long line when we got there, and we waited as one person after another in front of us carried away a small cup of steaming chocolate liquid. As each person passed, the cold seemed to bite even harder.

I hadn't been to a football game in the longest time. I used to go to the games every week to support Baylor, but when he'd graduated, I'd stopped coming. And this weather was just a big reminder why.

The game was almost over. The Westwood Cyclones were winning, which wasn't a surprise considering we were going against County Bees. Bees versus a Cyclone? They didn't stand a chance.

"I'm freezing," Adalia huffed, her breath turning to smoke in the cold. "Why didn't we bring blankets?"

"Because it's 'a matter of pride in our ability to endure,' which is what you said when I suggested bringing them before coming here," I replied, rolling my eyes and rubbing my hands together. I looked down at them before giving a slight smile. Liam had written *#14* on our hands with marker before the game. He wanted to know that we were cheering for him, which of course we were or else we wouldn't be here. But I couldn't deny that I had also been chasing someone else with my eyes for the majority of the game.

"What do you want?" a raspy voice asked, breaking me out of my trance as I noticed we had made our way to the front of the line.

Adalia tucked her hands in the pockets of Liam's jacket, which he'd given her to wear before the game and was huge on her, and responded eagerly, "Two hot chocolates, please."

"YOU'RE GOING TO STAY HERE?" Liam asked once the game finished. He looked around nervously, and I couldn't blame him for being anxious after what had happened with Adalia. I reassured him that I'd be fine and would call them if I needed help, and he finally gave in. "We'll wait for you in the car."

"Okay," I answered and then sent them both a quick wave as they walked out of sight, though with a hundred other people walking in the same direction, it wasn't long before they were blending into the crowd and I was being pushed against the fence.

I was waiting outside the changing rooms, praying to God that Kyler hadn't already left. I pulled out my phone and glanced at the time nervously. It was late, cold, and dark, none of which were appealing to me. I didn't want to stay out here any longer than I had to, especially not when paranoid thoughts were already circling my mind. I wondered if Ingrid had been in a similar situation before the murderer found her.

I kicked a pebble on the ground, hoping to distract myself

from my fear as I made my way toward the now closed concession stand. Then a distant clang came from behind me, and I snapped my head around.

Past the wire fence separating the field from the parking lot, I could just make out Sterling as he kicked a can out of his way. He was dressed in sweats, and his black hair looked rustled after having played football. Another man stood in front of him, but his back was turned to me, and I couldn't make out much aside from the fact that he was taller and had the same dark hair as Sterling.

Sterling frowned as he threw his hands around animatedly; he seemed like he was desperately trying to convince the other man of something. The man suddenly shouted something back before roughly pushing Sterling's chest.

Sterling fumbled backward, and I was surprised to see that he didn't look angry. Rather, his expression sank into frustration, maybe even defeat. He regained his balance just as the man began walking away, and Sterling scampered after him.

I stared at the place where they'd been. I was already a bit paranoid about Sterling, but the fact that he seemed so different, that he could get so flustered and even scared, was hard to comprehend when I was so used to seeing him with a gentle smile and a cool disposition. Who was he talking to? What kind of company did he keep? As I thought more about how odd that whole scenario had been, a hard, unfamiliar voice suddenly broke my trance.

"What are you doing here all by yourself?"

The hairs on my arm stuck up, and I gripped my phone tightly, almost afraid to look up and match the voice to its owner. His haircut was short and uneven. He gave a wicked smile, showing off a cut by his lip. Two other men stood next to him, leering at me with the same crazed eyes and grins. "Want to hang out?"

My heartbeat skyrocketed in my chest. My hand was shaking as I quickly brought my phone behind my back.

Was it already time to call someone? Would they even let me?

"I'm waiting on someone," I answered in a way that I hoped sounded indifferent. My breathing felt shallow as I talked, and the air became heavy in my throat. Scenarios ran in my head now. Should I make a run for it? I skimmed over their bodies; their legs were like bricks, all hard edges and rugged. I was smaller, but they were stronger, and I wasn't going to bet on being faster than them.

"Are you sure? I bet we're better company," the second one chimed in in a low voice. I took a step back, frowning at them before looking away. I tried to stay composed, but I felt like a cornered rabbit, red eyes darting in fear. "What are you looking at? Our eyes are here, dollface."

"Sorry, it's too dark to see anything," I sputtered, now in panic mode. It wasn't just my paranoia this time.

I tried my best to position my phone to my side, my eyes shifting toward the screen then back at the men. I didn't want to draw more attention than I needed to.

"Yeah?" the first man growled, his eyes squinting. "Wanna go somewhere with more light, then?"

"Actually, I have to go," I said, turning my back to them and taking a step away. My finger was just about to hit the Call button for Liam when one of the men grabbed a handful of my hair and jerked me back in their direction.

The third one, the tallest and scariest-looking one, turned me around, swatted my phone to the ground, and gave a laugh that made me cringe. "You should've just said yes. Inviting some friends?"

No. No, no, no. This wasn't happening. My hand frantically dug into my purse and tightened around a small device. Pepper spray.

"You can't hear?" he asked.

I willed my hand not to shake. I'd never used it before, but Liam had. I knew it covered a lot of ground, I just had to point it in the right direction. Although if I sprayed myself, they'd probably feel it too.

"Let me go," I almost whimpered. I had to. I had to do it. Now wasn't the time to hesitate.

"But we're having so much fun." The second one gave a shattering grin, and I tried to force down any tears that might've surfaced. "Just cooperate."

"Just leave me alone!" I shouted, pulling out the gray container of pepper spray. I shut my eyes tightly, about to spray in their direction, but suddenly there was a loud crack.

My eyes flashed open.

"You heard her. Leave," a voice I recognized said from beside me. Kyler shook out his hand and looked down cruelly at the man who'd taken the hit. His nose was bleeding. I almost couldn't believe it as I scampered closer to Kyler, feeling better now that my hair was free of their grasp.

My eyes narrowed harshly at the three thugs.

"You," the first one spat. He turned his head so that light shone against coarse cheeks, and a brief flash of surprise overtook

Kyler's expression. "You're going to regret that, Fellan. You just made a big mistake."

Kyler almost winced. His eyes burned in outrage, and it seemed like he was using all the restraint he had not to throw an insult at the men.

"Mind your own business," one of them finally said, but he scowled and gestured with his head toward the exit. "Let's go. This just got annoying."

The other two grunted in agreement before shooting me looks that could kill and then disappearing past the fence. When I knew they were gone, my lips finally stopped quivering.

I began to turn toward Kyler, but I didn't make it very far before his hands were rough against my shoulders and I was being guided up against the fence. It didn't hurt; even in his frustration, he was still gentle.

"What the hell were you thinking? Why were you out here alone?" he began, his grip tensing around my shoulders. His voice was loud, hoarse, but it became quieter each time he spoke. "Are you okay?"

"Yeah," I almost whispered. I didn't want to think about what might have happened if he hadn't been here. I was grateful for the pepper spray, but I had hesitated too long. I felt weak, pathetic, especially in front of the one who'd been avoiding me. "I was waiting for you."

Kyler continued to stare at me in disbelief before frowning again. "You should've called for someone."

"I was going to, but . . ." I nodded my head toward my phone. It lay alone on the blacktop, just a few feet away. Kyler seemed to grasp the situation before reaching down and placing the device in my hand. "I had pepper spray."

He must have noticed how my hand shook as I put it away. Now that it was just us, the fear was starting to catch up to me. No more adrenaline raced through my veins. My eyes stung with tears, and Kyler quickly averted his gaze.

"Yeah," was all he said. I wished he would say more. If he didn't start talking, I knew my nerves would get the better of me, and I wasn't prepared to start sniffling like an idiot in front of him. Especially since I'd waited here to confront him.

A cold breeze suddenly ran through my hair, and I crossed my arms.

"Put it on. It's cold," Kyler said, throwing me a gray hoodie.

I didn't protest. It was too cold.

I slid it over my torso and onto my arms. It was warm, and it was his. I looked back up at him, but when he didn't say anything, I finally spoke up. "You knew them."

"No, I didn't," he lied while tucking his hands into the pockets of his pants. Steam left his lips every time he said a word.

"I'm not stupid. I saw your face," I said, aiming a small scowl at him. I couldn't focus on what had just happened; I didn't want to break down. I'd waited here for a reason, and I was going to get to the bottom of it now. "Is this part of why you're suddenly ignoring me?"

His eyes widened for a second at that question, but he didn't deny it. Then Kyler sighed before turning to look at me.

"I told you to trust me."

"What happened to us working together?" I muttered, tossing my head. It was dark all around us. The blazing stadium lights were turned off now, but having Kyler next to me made me forget, just for a second, how scary the dark could be.

He didn't respond for a while. Instead, he threw himself against the fence next to me, letting his head fall back and hit it. The seconds ticked on like hours. Long hours that only seemed extended in the breeze.

"I'm sorry," he said.

"Are you?" I asked in a voice that was barely above a whisper. I surprised myself a little by asking so quickly, so automatically. I wanted to believe him, wanted to believe that maybe I mattered as much to him as he did to me.

"Yeah," Kyler replied, his eyes looking down in what almost seemed like shame. "I'm sorry for ignoring you without saying anything. I shouldn't have done that."

"Yeah, you shouldn't have," I agreed.

He let out a half laugh, and I shot a glare his way. "It's not because I want to ignore you. It's because . . ." He shook his head. "It's complicated right now, Brynn. Just trust me."

"How am I supposed to trust you when you won't tell me anything?" My voice came out bitter as my shoulders sank. Of course, things would turn out like this. Nothing had been easy lately, and I was a fool for expecting anything different.

He didn't answer, so I looked him over and continued. "Do you know why I waited for you?"

"I have an idea," he said, his deep voice harsh against the sound of the night. His eyes were intent on mine. "Why did you?"

"Because I'm mad at you. After everything we've been working on together . . . and after what just happened to Adalia . . ." I started softly. This wasn't the best time for me to lose a pillar of support. Especially not one that I liked this much. "You have bad timing when it comes to ghosting someone, you know?" I spat, tears of frustration threatening my eyes. I looked away and sniffled.

"Brynn," he said. The way he said my name sounded almost pained, and I was glad he was hurting too. "I . . . I can't make any excuses. I'm sorry."

"Stop that," I grumbled. "Stop saying you're sorry."

He looked at me in silence, and it made me even more upset.

"You could've said something. You could've texted me saying 'We're over' or at least given an explanation. You said to trust you, but you won't even answer my messages. You're not giving me any new information, either, so what are you doing?" My cheeks were so warm with anger that I couldn't feel the cold.

His eyes widened as he opened his mouth to say something. Then he stopped and decided against it.

"What?" I said with a frown.

He ran his hand through his hair and made a small noise of frustration. "You're unrelenting, you know that, Brynn?"

"So you've said," I murmured.

"I can't say what I want to say right now," he said, his blue eyes pleading. They still seemed to glow despite how dim and frigid it was around us. "Wait until I'm done, and I'll tell you everything."

My anger morphed into confusion. "Done?"

"I'll explain everything once I'm done," he repeated.

"Done with what?"

He shook his head. "I can't tell you. Not yet. Just . . . trust me, okay?"

I didn't. Not after this stunt he'd pulled.

If he wasn't going to tell me, I'd figure it out myself.

CHAPTER TWELVE

AFTER I'D CONFRONTED KYLER, he'd made sure I got back to Liam's car safely. Everything about the situation was sketchy. It didn't feel like a breakup, not that we'd actually been dating, but still . . . I wanted to know what was going on with him. I was beyond mad, but now that I'd heard directly from him, that anger turned into suspicion.

What was he up to, and why couldn't he tell me?

The next day, Adalia, Liam, and I sat together during lunch like we always did, and I told them what had happened. "It just came out of nowhere," I said. "One second we were fine, and the next he's completely ignoring me. I know he's ghosting me, but I think there's more to it than that. He basically said he can't tell me why, like it's not safe for me to know what's going on. I don't get it. "

Liam shook his head exaggeratedly and tutted. "The first stage of grief is denial, Brynn."

My eyes rolled so hard I was surprised they didn't fall out. "You are so not helping right now. I know when to give up, okay?" Well, maybe not. "If circumstances were different, and we didn't live in a town with murderers running around, I would take the hint and back off. But this is what we're dealing with."

Adalia nodded. "You're right. Things are weird right now." She looked down and frowned. "Actually, I have some more news."

Liam and I shared a look. "Good or bad?" he asked.

"I guess both," she said. Her voice was defeated. "I'm so sick of always bringing the mood down with my problems. I'm sorry."

"What? Ad, we've never thought that before. You're not bringing the mood down. I'd feel worse if you didn't tell us anything," I said, sitting up in my seat. "Don't feel bad about that. Ever."

Liam nodded. "She took the words right out of my mouth."

Adalia gave a faint smile. "Thanks. Well . . . I talked to my dad again. I told him that if our money problems had anything to do with my kidnapping, he needed to tell me. And . . . he did. He broke down crying." She stiffened. "I'd never seen him like that before. I mean, I've never seen him cry before."

Her fingers tangled together as she glanced down. "He told me he has a gambling problem."

My eyes went wide. "What?"

"Yeah. He didn't tell me details, but my parents talked it over, and they think it's a good idea if I live with my mom until everything gets figured out."

Liam's eyes darkened. "You're moving to St. Louis?"

Adalia gave a slow nod.

It was obvious we all wanted to protest. We couldn't say

anything, though, since it was probably the right thing to do. I didn't want her to get hurt. I knew Liam didn't either. But having her that far away was going to be rough. We also didn't know how long things would take to get better, which meant she could be gone anywhere from a week to years.

Liam's head hung just a little. He must've been thinking similar thoughts as me.

"Do you know when?" I asked.

"Well, we're still figuring out the dates. I think it'll be sometime next week, but I don't know exactly." She ran her hands over her pants. "Sorry, I . . . I don't really want to go, but I'm also scared."

"Don't be sorry, Ad," Liam said, placing his hand over hers. He gave her a sincere look. "I think it's a good idea."

"You do?" She sounded hurt.

Liam's eyes widened, and he tightened his hand around hers. "No, I mean . . . I don't want you to leave. But I don't want you to get hurt either. That would be worse."

"Yeah," I said. "You shouldn't have to feel scared to come to school or even go outside. I know that whole thing was so traumatizing. Maybe it'll be a good, short break."

At least I hoped it would be short.

"Yeah. You're right." Adalia gave a smile. "Thanks, guys."

I returned her smile. "Did he say how his gambling issue was connected to your kidnapping?"

She shook her head. "It was really hard to understand him. He was kind of a mess, and I . . . I just felt uncomfortable prying while he was like that."

"That makes sense," Liam said. "You probably—" His words

suddenly cut off as his dark eyes caught on something, and he gasped. "Whoa."

When I followed his gaze, I almost gasped too.

Kyler.

As he walked into the cafeteria, half-hidden by Sterling, I could make out red blotches around his cheekbones and lips. They looked painful, and I had to resist getting up and going to him.

He caught my eye for just a second before glancing quickly away, and I frowned. What was he doing? His walk was slower than usual, and I wondered if he had more bruises underneath his clothes.

"That's it," I muttered.

Adalia and Liam both turned my way in surprise.

"I'm going to figure this out," I declared. "I know it's risky, but I need to find out what's going on. For the sake of you, Adalia, and for Kyler."

"But how?" Liam's eyebrows knit together. "I don't want you to get hurt either."

I shook my head. "I won't. Because I'll have you guys."

IT WAS DARK when I pulled into the near-empty parking lot. Even my Jeep, which was normally glistening white, seemed shadowy in the unfamiliar environment.

I ducked my head to get a better glimpse out the front window of my car, but the only view my eyes were met with was a looming black warehouse just a few feet ahead of me. Faded graffiti etched the walls, and empty plastic bags blew in the wind, littering the already dirty sidewalk.

With a frown etched into my features, I pulled out my phone and double-checked the address. Adalia and Liam had agreed to help me follow Kyler after school; they'd trailed him from a distance and let me know when he finally stopped.

This was a weird final destination.

Adalia and Liam were parked down a couple streets with my location on. They'd be ready to come at a moment's notice and save me if anything went wrong.

My hands trembled.

The silence seemed consuming as I shut off my car. When I stepped out of my Jeep, the cold wrapped around my body like a blanket, and I pulled my jacket tighter around my torso. I tried not to recall the fear I'd felt at the football game, that helplessness and panic. My eyes shut tight as I buried it down. It wouldn't be like that.

I had nothing to fear. Adalia and Liam were with me this time.

My foot crushed a shattered bottle as I walked closer to the warehouse. I'd never entered this part of town before. The ground was littered with cigarette butts as well as other trash I didn't want to spend time identifying. The hoot of a bird pierced the blackened sky.

I texted my friends with numb fingers as I made my way around the building. As I turned the corner, I could make out a shine of light reflected on the ground. It was pale against the grainy dirt it lit up.

I continued walking, a little slower so as not to draw attention to myself, before a voice came from the direction of the room. I stopped.

"Look, I don't want to do this," a familiar deep voice echoed. It was still a distance away from me. "Just tell me why you don't have the money. I'll even put away the gun."

My body froze. Gun?

I was about to turn on my heel when the voice spoke again.

"Glaring at me like that isn't gonna help anyone. Let's just get this over with, yeah? Where is it?" he said from inside the room. I couldn't believe it. The closer I got, the more familiar the voice became, and I had to accept the fact that it was Kyler. The disconnect in my head confused me; how could he be speaking those words?

I couldn't see who he was talking to or how many people were in there with him, so I decided to find out.

Despite all the alarms firing off in my head, I continued on in my pursuit, making sure my boots didn't crunch against any glass or dead leaves on the ground. I could hear a thumping in my head as my blood rushed in fear, but I couldn't ignore what was going on.

"I know you won't shoot me." A shaky, older voice came from the entrance. I tried to calm myself. I was right next to the open garage door.

"True," Kyler said. I peeked my head into the space, and the sight I saw made me hold in a gasp.

Shivers brushed up my arm. What the hell was I watching? I knew Kyler was up to something, but this?

Kyler twirled a gun in his fingers as he stood in front of an older man who'd been loosely tied to a small chair. It was obvious that the man could have escaped whenever he wanted. Kyler seemed confident that he wouldn't due to the weapon in his hand.

"I won't kill you. You're right about that. But," he paused, letting the seriousness of the situation sink in, "what about the rest of your family?"

I tried to ignore how my knees turned weak. I should've hidden, turned back, but I hadn't been able to move from my spot. I stood at the entrance, just one foot inside, while the rest of my body felt unstable. This wasn't the Kyler I knew. I needed to find out more.

Suddenly, the old man's wide eyes met mine, and I tried to turn back to my previous spot, but Kyler was quick to catch on. His head flashed over his shoulder with his gun pointed outward, yet as soon as his gaze landed on me, the gun fell to the floor with an echoing clank.

There was a pause. No one breathed. No one moved.

His arms were still extended outward, yet his blue eyes looked darker than they usually did. When he spoke, his voice was unbelieving. "What are you doing here?"

"What's going on?" I asked instead, my voice wavering.

This didn't make any sense.

Kyler had been working with me to figure all this out. How could he be a part of it? Had he been messing with me this whole time?

Tears of frustration started welling in my eyes as I tried to calm down my breathing and process the situation.

There was no way this was right.

My hands balled into shaking fists. They shook from disbelief at myself, at Kyler, at everything. Tears trickled down my cheeks, and I tried desperately to wipe them away with my fingers.

"Shit, no," his hoarse voice said as he rushed toward me. I

tried to keep my eyes averted, but he ducked down and made sure I was looking at him. His eyebrows were creased in frantic worry as his eyes pleaded with mine. "It's not what you're thinking."

I didn't say anything, but I didn't need to because the sound of a chair being pushed backward got both of our attention as the man clambered forward, grasping for the fallen gun with panicked eyes. It was in his shaking hands, and he pointed it at us.

"Get down!" Kyler shouted. He tugged my arm down at the same time as the gun went off; we crashed against the floor. I saw white lights flash against my eyelids as I lifted my head with a grimace, but Kyler was already sitting up as the other man ran toward another exit. Kyler stood up with lightning speed and took a step in the man's direction before suddenly pausing and glancing down at me. Our eyes locked, but I pulled away.

He threw his head back and took a deep breath before crouching down beside me. Then he ran his thumb across my tear-stained cheek. "Are you hurt?"

I shook my head and felt his hand press against my back as he came and sat next to me. My head throbbed with a dull headache as I looked down at my lit-up phone.

Are you okay? We heard a noise.
Do you want us to come?

"Wait, Brynn," Kyler said. "Let me explain. Please."

I shot him a glare but couldn't bring myself to do more. He'd said to wait until he was done. Done with this?

I texted them back.

"You get ten minutes before I tell Ad and Li to come." I kept my gaze hard and my voice even.

He nodded. His pale face was an indication of how exhausted he was, and the red spots I'd noticed earlier were turning darker now.

"Thanks," he said in a whisper. Kyler paused thoughtfully, as if trying to figure out how to explain everything within the time limit I'd given him. I knew it would be hard, and a longer conversation would likely be necessary, but I needed answers now.

"God." He chuckled to himself. "This looks so bad."

I nodded.

"Just to get it out there," he said, turning toward me. "This was a recent development."

I furrowed my eyebrows, and he continued. "After you told me what happened with Adalia, it got me thinking about Sterling. You were right. Something was off about him, so I got him to talk. Under one condition."

"What?" I asked.

"That I'd join him. There's this organization run by his older brother. They lure people into these gambling rings, take all their money, and then act like loan sharks—the worst kind. They just keep adding interest. They never stop. And their victims can't even report them because they're part of the illegal gambling."

I almost couldn't believe what he was saying. Gambling rings alone were dangerous, but when organized crime got involved, people got hurt. Or killed, as we had already seen.

"Wait," I said suddenly. My voice was edged with concern.

"Kyler, you . . . you joined? Why?"

His eyes darkened as he looked at me. I'd never seen his gaze so sharp before. "I had to. You can only learn so much through rumors. Plus, we've already come so far. I wanted to get answers, and it didn't sit well with me knowing Sterling was in on it."

"But how did you know he was involved?" I asked.

"When you told me about Adalia getting kidnapped and that the guy looked like Sterling, it made more sense than I wanted it to. Lately, Sterling's been acting kind of weird. Like he keeps flashing money, paying for everyone when we go out for food, that kind of thing. He acts like a different person now . . . over-confident and secretive at the same time."

"What did you say to him?"

"I brought up the incident with Adalia, just to see his reaction, but it was weird. He sounded frustrated about it, and when I called him out, we made a deal. He said he'd tell me anything I wanted to know if I joined him. I couldn't say no, not when he'd already told me there was something going on and that he was a part of it, so I agreed. I didn't know what I was joining, but . . . it's a lot."

I shook my head. "This is too dangerous. Way too dangerous."

He gave me a flirtatious smile before tilting his head. "Are you worried about me?"

"No," I said sternly. I couldn't believe he was acting like this, not when my hands were still shaking from the shock that came with being shot at. "Stop it. You're . . . you're unbelievable. What are you going to do if they actually make you use that gun, Kyler? And your face . . ."

My eyebrows creased in worry as I brushed my trembling

fingers against the red marks on his cheeks. "You're already hurt."

Then the realization hit me.

You're going to regret that, Fellan. You just made a big mistake.

"Those guys at the football game did this, didn't they?" I asked. My shoulders shook at the anger I felt. How could people be so disgusting?

"It doesn't matter," Kyler said dismissively. He took my hand and laced our fingers together like it was the most natural thing in the world, like that was how it was supposed to be.

"It does! How could you let them hit you?"

"I just joined. Sterling has been vouching for me, but I'm still at the bottom of the chain. I punched them, which means they get to retaliate." He sighed and looked around the warehouse room. "Even this was an initiation test."

I blinked. "Initiation? Into the gang?"

He nodded, and I felt my blood drain.

"And you failed. Because of me."

"I didn't fail," Kyler said quickly. "I was supposed to let him go after threatening him. Even the gun in my hand was just a threat." That explained why the ropes had been so loose.

"So you won't get in trouble?" I asked, relief flooding my words.

"No, as long as they don't find out about you. I don't think that'll happen, though. Not when that guy looked so shaken up." Kyler's eyes lingered on the fallen chair, his expression sullen. I felt bad for that man too. Being threatened with your family was something I couldn't imagine.

"What about the gun he took?" I asked.

"I . . ." He paused. "I don't know. I'll tell them I accidentally dropped it in a gutter or something. They won't believe me, but they'll probably just think I lied to keep it for myself. A lot of guys do that."

The fact that he was associating himself with those kinds of people now made my stomach tense up. I couldn't stand this. I didn't want him risking his safety like this—it was too dangerous, and that was coming from me. Finally, I asked him the question that bothered me the most. "Why didn't you tell me?" My voice came out quiet.

"Huh?"

"Why didn't you tell me you joined? You could have texted me or . . ." My words got caught in my throat.

"I couldn't. I think my phone is being tracked, so I didn't want them seeing you or your number anywhere."

Tracking his phone? The concept made me shiver.

"Then what about the locker notes?"

Kyler's head shook. "Sterling's watching me closely now. It would've been too risky, especially since we have practice together. I didn't want them to think you had anything to do with me. It's fine if I get hurt, but you're a different story, Brynn." When I didn't reply, he drew closer. "I'll find out everything for us, okay? We'll figure everything out."

I balled up my free hand. "I don't like this, Kyler. Any of it."

"I'll be careful. I promise." He squeezed my hand reassuringly, but it didn't help. "In and out."

I wanted to argue more, but I didn't.

CHAPTER THIRTEEN

I SPENT THE NEXT DAY AT SCHOOL processing everything and worrying. I couldn't believe how reckless Kyler was being, and I was still slightly mad that he'd ghosted me to join a gang.

I knew it had been for my safety, but it was still annoying. Since I had gym third period, it was the perfect time to stop by the locker and write him a note. I knew he'd told me not to text him because he suspected they were tracking his phone, which didn't make me feel any better about the situation, so I drafted a note and threw it in just before gym class.

Come over today after school so
we can figure things out.

I knew he wouldn't like it. The circumstances hadn't changed just because I'd found out, and his reasons for avoiding me still stood, but I didn't care. He couldn't do this alone.

When I went about my daily habit of checking the locker after school, I wasn't surprised to see Kyler there waiting for me on his side of the locker wall.

"Brynn," he said and gave a sigh of relief. Then he held up my note. "I can't. You know that. I don't want them knowing we're still—"

I shook my head. "I don't care about that. You made the stupid decision to . . ." I glanced around the room and lowered my voice. "You don't have any help. We're doing this together now."

When he hesitated, I leaned in. His eyes stuck to mine, and I could feel my eyes widen as I pleaded. "Please, Kyler. I can't just sit still worrying about you."

Finally, he gave in. "All right. I get it. I'll come after practice."

"Good," I said. "And, Kyler?"

He rose his eyebrow.

"I'm still mad at you." And it was true. If I hadn't made the decision to follow him last night, he still wouldn't have told me anything.

Kyler scratched the back of his head awkwardly before he rose. His sigh echoed against the lockers.

"I know."

WHEN I OPENED THE FRONT DOOR TO MY HOUSE, Kyler stood stiffly, his confidence minuscule in comparison to his usual flirty disposition. It almost made me happy.

"Hey," I said.

"Hey," he repeated. His brown hair was disheveled, and a hint of pink still tinted his cheeks from practice. He shoved his hands in the pockets of his sweatpants as he looked down at me, and I wanted to curse myself for thinking he was cute.

"Come in," I said as I stepped out of the way. He put his hand behind his head as he stepped in, glancing around the living room with intent eyes. "You can sit there if you want." I pointed to the couch that faced the TV, and he let himself sink into the cushions.

"Were you doing homework?" he asked, his eyes trailing from the papers on the coffee table to me as I sat to the right of him. Kyler's smile seemed shy and playful at the same time.

"Oh . . . yeah," I said. "Kind of. It was hard to concentrate. Homework seems kind of pointless when everything else is happening." I turned to look at his face. The bruises were now edging purple, and I had to resist staring. My hand inched closer to his cheek, but I held back. "Where else did you get hit?"

He shifted his gaze away. "Mostly on my face," he said flippantly. I knew he was lying, but before I could say anything, he held his hand up. The knuckles of his fingers were bruised, and I realized he must have gotten those the night he saved me. A tiny bit of my anger subsided as he grinned my way. "I got to help you and punch them at the same time. It was worth it."

"You think so?"

Kyler raised his hand up toward the ceiling light, and I let my eyes run over every line. "Yeah," he said. Then he took a breath. "I couldn't focus during practice today. I was trying to think of what to say to you . . . how to apologize." His eyebrows furrowed in thought as his words spilled out. "I know I'm being stupid, Brynn. That's the reason I didn't want to get you involved, but I should've known you'd find out on your own. I shouldn't have joined impulsively, not without talking to you first. We're a team, and I . . . I guess I got scared. When you told me what happened with Adalia, it reminded me how serious this is. How possible it is that you could get hurt. I don't know what I'd do if . . ." His words trailed off, and he looked away.

"That's how I feel about you too," I said.

"Yeah?" Kyler chuckled in surprise.

I frowned. "Yeah," I said. "It doesn't make me happy knowing that the chances of you getting hurt are higher now. Way higher."

"I'll be okay. Better me than you," Kyler said so softly I thought I'd imagined it. Then he reached out and let a loose strand of my hair fall between his fingers. His voice was low when he spoke again. "I'm sorry for ghosting you."

"Good."

He placed his forearms on top of his legs before leaning over. "You know, that night at the football game, you said I should've just texted you, 'We're over.' But I couldn't. I know it was selfish of me, but I can't let you go. I couldn't explain either." He sighed. "I didn't know what to do. If I said anything, that would mean it really was over, and . . ." He paused, his hands reaching for mine. His voice took on a hoarse edge. "That would've hurt more than anything."

I couldn't find it in me to be upset anymore. Not when the boy I liked so much was here, bruised and in pain, explaining his actions so desperately to me.

"Brynn." His low voice was enough to draw me toward him. Then his lips were on my knuckles and he was looking up with a glint in his eye.

I froze at the sight. He was so attractive I almost wanted to sigh. He edged closer, his face just an inch away as he spoke again. "Forgive me."

His free hand traced against my leg as he shifted forward, and I tried not to squirm under his touch. He must have realized the effect he had on me as his lips grazed my ear and curled into a smirk.

"Please?"

I couldn't take all his teasing, and when his lips brushed against my neck, heat spiraled through my veins.

"Kyler," I gasped. I hadn't kissed him since the party, and now he was trailing his lips against my bare skin, against places that he'd never touched before. It felt so natural somehow, and I knew that being apart had made both of us more starved for each other than I wanted to admit.

"Say you'll forgive me," he said again, his timbre low, hypnotizing. Then his lips were behind my ear, planting kisses all the way down my neck, stopping just above my collarbone. My breathing was heavy as I glanced down to see his lashes fanned across his face as he concentrated on me.

"I forgive you." My voice came out as a whisper.

Kyler's flushed face backed away from my neck, and he grinned. "Yeah?"

"Yeah." I nodded. His glazed eyes trailed down my face slowly until his gaze finally stopped on my mouth.

His thumb ran over my lips, first the top, then the bottom, which he tugged down ever so slightly. His eyes half closed as he came nearer, and when they held mine and I didn't move away, he knew I was giving him permission.

Then his lips were against mine in a wave of heat and desire, the same feelings that ran in my blood as he traced his hand against my neck. My head tilted in response, my lips parting for him as he clutched the back of the couch behind me and leaned over my body. I grasped his soft hair between my fingers as I steadied myself against him. His hand slid down, palming my back and raising my hips to meet his as he got closer and closer, as close as we could get.

He deepened the kiss, and a low moan sounded against my mouth as I parted my lips farther. He tasted like salt.

My hands slipped under his shirt and trailed against sweat and muscle. His eyes fluttered open before he gave me a lopsided smile and pressed his lips under my jaw.

"Kyler," I gasped. He trailed another kiss on my neck. "You're too good at this."

His hand cupped my face before he brought his lips to my nose. Even that kiss felt hot, regardless of how chaste it was.

"It's your fault." He tapped our foreheads together. His blue eyes that normally shone were darker now, reflecting an image of my flushed face. "You make me so desperate, Brynn."

I kissed him again.

He made me desperate too.

ABOUT AN HOUR LATER, I sat between Kyler's legs on the couch. His hands held mine, minuscule compared to his, as he ran his thumb up and down against the sides. It felt so comfortable that I was tempted to lie back against his chest and fall asleep.

We hadn't gone too far. We'd kissed . . . and a little more, but it was just the right amount. I'd missed him, and it was nice to finally get a moment to ourselves. Birds chirped outside the window as the sun set. A faint orange glow lit up Kyler's face, and I wanted to kiss him again.

Too bad we had to talk about infiltrating a gang.

"My next step is to get evidence," Kyler said. I could feel his chest rumble from behind me as he talked. "I haven't gotten a chance yet, but now that I passed initiation, I have more access."

I turned around to look at him in surprise and relief. "You passed?"

He smiled. "Yeah. Sterling pulled some strings."

Although I hated Sterling for what his group had done to Adalia, and maybe others, I was at least thankful he seemed to be looking out for Kyler. It was still a mystery to me how Kyler felt about Sterling—was he using him or did he still consider him a friend?

I hoped it was the first option, but I knew deep down Kyler wasn't the type of person who could just flip a switch like that, not about someone he'd cared about.

"So, once you get enough evidence, should we go to the police?" It sounded logical, but my limited experience with the police in this city had not been great. I didn't trust them.

Kyler shook his head. "No. There are some cops that are in on everything. They know about the gambling and the loan sharks . . . everything. Not all the cops, but some of them. Enough for us to be wary."

I frowned as he took my hand and began to trace the outline of my fingers. It was such a soothing action compared to what we were talking about. "So, then who should we talk to? Who's above the cops?"

Kyler shrugged. "I was thinking maybe the FBI. We need

enough evidence to take this case to them."

Chills ran up my arms at the thought. I should have realized how serious this situation was when I'd first gotten involved, especially since it was a murder that had triggered my involvement. Still, it didn't feel real.

Two teenagers taking on a gang?

I had to stay hopeful.

"Okay." I gave a firm nod. "You collect evidence. I'll decipher it. We still don't know how gambling ties into Ingrid's death or Adalia's kidnapping."

"You're right. I'll try to get some more information."

"Kyler," I said. When I faced him, my expression was hard. "Be careful. I'm serious. Be more than careful."

He planted a kiss on my forehead.

"I'm being careful. I promise."

CHAPTER FOURTEEN

ALMOST A WEEK HAD GONE BY since Kyler and I had agreed to gather evidence. He'd been doing a good job with it, which made me grateful but also nervous. Baylor was also making me nervous—ever since the weekend Adalia had been kidnapped, he'd been texting me a lot more, and on his last couple weekend visits he'd seemed worried. He'd even asked if he could come down during the week rather than wait for the weekend, but I'd shot that idea down. Kyler and I needed to focus, and having Baylor, who caught onto things too quickly, around would just make things a lot harder than they already were.

My parents also seemed concerned, but I guessed that was normal considering their only daughter had witnessed a murder. Our calls were usually lighthearted, though, and they never pushed me to talk more than I wanted to.

While sitting at my desk in second period, a text notification came from my phone, and I sighed. Unfortunately, Baylor was not like my parents.

Are you still hanging out with that Sterling kid?

No.

Good.

I loved Baylor with my whole heart, but he could be a bit much when it came to being an overprotective brother.

There were still a few minutes before class started, so I scrolled idly before I felt a tap on my shoulder and heard Kyler's voice from behind. "Hey."

I turned back just a little, replying in the same monotone voice. "Hey."

By this point, we'd put enough effort into making the school think we were just exes that it wasn't abnormal to see us having a conversation. The reason we'd stopped "dating" originally was to avoid being linked to each other by Ingrid's killer. Now enough time had passed that Kyler and I didn't seem close anymore—we just had the same kind of "friendly acquaintance" relationship he had with most of the people at this school.

"Did you do your homework?" he asked.

"Yeah?"

"Can I have answer five?"

I rolled my eyes, trying to put on a show for anyone who happened to see us. Then I dug through my binder and pulled out the assignment. I wasn't sure if he actually needed the homework or if he was just trying to act like it, but considering all that he was doing with Sterling, I wouldn't have been surprised if he really was struggling to catch up on schoolwork.

I passed the paper back. "Just give it back before class starts," I said, and he gave a nod.

"Thanks," Kyler said.

We didn't talk again that hour.

AFTER MORNING CLASSES WERE OVER, I was happy to be in the company of my friends.

I looked over at Liam and Adalia from the microwave I stood at. We were sitting in a different part of the cafeteria, one that was more hidden.

Adalia munched on an apple slice, and Liam leaned back in his chair as he looked at her. She'd been chewing on that slice for a while, which made the both of us wonder what was on her mind. Finally, she asked, "What if I don't make any friends in St. Louis?"

Liam frowned. "Are you serious? You're the most friendly person I know." Then he pondered. "Aside from me, I guess."

She laughed and hit his arm playfully. "Seriously, Li?"

He smiled back at her. "You won't have any problems."

At the microwave's beep, I took out my container of leftover pasta and slid into the seat next to them. "He's right," I added. "You'll be totally fine. Do you have a specific date yet?"

Her green eyes fell. "Yeah," she said in a low voice. "It's sooner than I was hoping for." Adalia's head drooped. "I'm taking off this weekend. My mom's gonna pick me up from the airport Sunday night."

Liam stiffened next to me. "That's so soon."

"Yeah," she mumbled. "It sucks. I don't want to go, but also . . ."

"Don't worry," I said encouragingly. "We're going to figure everything out. Make this place safe again. You'll be back before you know it."

Adalia's smile was brighter this time. "I'm so glad my best friend is a detective."

Liam and I both laughed at that.

The mood settled back into a playful one, but I noticed from the corner of my eye that Liam's face suddenly looked determined.

The two of them continued to talk, and I would've joined, but Kyler caught my eye as he walked to his table with Sterling. I didn't love the fact that he had to keep hanging around Sterling, especially since we both knew he was involved in sketchy activities. They took their seats, and only a couple minutes passed before I saw two girls stand up from their table and walk toward them. Though they were talking to both Sterling and Kyler, it was obvious they were more interested in Kyler; they'd laugh at everything he said, and he seemed surprised, like he wasn't trying to be funny. I finally had to peel my eyes away before I got too jealous.

I wanted to do something, but I couldn't. We were broken up, and even though we talked in class sometimes, it was still a bummer not being able to act close during school. It was even more of a bummer watching other girls flirt with him now that he was "single."

We weren't even dating—we never had been—but we were still something.

I sighed and took a bite of my pasta before throwing one more look his way.

Luckily, the girls were gone, and when Kyler caught my eye, he smiled.

THE NEXT MORNING, I was walking half-asleep in the school parking lot when I heard a door slam loudly farther down the lot.

As I squinted my eyes in the direction of the sound, I was surprised to see Adalia looking very unsettled as she moved away from a car, almost tripping in her haste. Not just any car, but Liam's car.

He didn't watch her get out. Instead, he ran his hands over his face and slammed the back of his head against the seat in frustration.

I paused just outside the front doors of the school when Adalia made eye contact with me, and immediately her eyes flashed in recognition. Then she was tumbling toward me, her arms outstretched as she collided with my chest and wrapped her arms around my torso.

"Whoa." I let out a gasp. "Adalia? What's—"

"What is Liam thinking? I can't believe he . . ." She groaned in frustration, snuggling her head closer to me. I gave her a pat on the head before trying to figure out the situation in a calm way.

"Hey, it's okay, Ad. What's wrong? I'm sure everything's going to be all right," I said in my best attempt at being soothing. I must have been a lot worse at it than I thought because just as I finished my sentence, she let out a heart-wrenching sob. "Adalia, I can't help you unless I know what's going on. Hey, just look at me for a second, okay?"

She followed my directions, her tear-stained emerald eyes downcast as she mumbled the cause of her outburst.

"Liam just confessed he has feelings for me. He said that now I was leaving, there wasn't any reason to hold back. He said he's liked me since he asked me out with that bug! In, like, third grade!" Her cheeks were flushed as she yelled and sniffled.

She shook her head, a frown imprinted in her brow. "What is he thinking?"

I was surprised at Adalia's reaction to the news. I had imagined Liam confessing to her before, sure, but the version in my head had been a bit different. It didn't involve tears or slamming doors.

I looked up and caught Liam's glance through the window of his car, but he gave me a smile and a shrug that pretty much said, "What's a guy to do?" I shrugged back and looked down, giving Adalia's head one more pat.

Finally, Adalia looked up with another sniff. "I'm going to the bathroom. I need to fix all of this," she gestured to her face, "before first period."

"Okay," I said, trying my best to sound supportive. "I'll meet you in class."

She gave me a weak nod before disappearing into the school's entrance doors. I felt bad for her, but I knew Liam would probably be hurting, too, so I sent him a quick text asking for a summary and offering some support. Then I took a step toward the school door, and Kyler's voice suddenly emerged next to me.

"Is Adalia all right?" Kyler asked.

"What?"

"I saw that little scene a few minutes ago," he elaborated, giving a small grin as my confused expression wore off. "Is she okay?"

"Oh. Yeah. Well, actually . . . " I gave a small sigh and held my phone so we could both see. He squinted his eyes as he leaned over to get a better look.

This sucks.

Ad, don't say that.

It does. I wish I was in St. Louis right now.

That would make me sad.

I'm sad too.

Kyler's expression was surprised as he turned back to me. "What happened?"

"You've seen her and Liam together," I said.

He nodded.

"Well, Liam likes her. I'm kind of surprised that she couldn't tell, but apparently she didn't know. Or, maybe she did. I have theories. Anyway, it doesn't matter because Liam told her himself."

Kyler frowned in confusion. "So what's the issue here?"

"They've been friends since elementary school. Adalia is really comfortable with him, like, he's her sense of safety, you know? She thinks it'll go down the drain if they date and it doesn't work out. I think she's just scared of losing him. Especially now, with everything going on."

"Oh, I get it," he said, clicking his tongue before leaning a little closer to me. "I wonder what Liam is going to do."

"Me too."

It was Thursday, and Liam and Adalia still weren't talking.

Liam was popular enough, so not being able to sit with us at lunch wasn't an issue for him. But it bothered me because not being together during Adalia's final days felt wrong. Adalia poked at her food and barely ate any of it. Every once in a while, I'd catch her staring longingly toward the football team's table, then snapping herself out of it and focusing back down on her apple slices.

The situation was getting out of hand, so on the way home from school, I pulled over and called Liam.

After a few rings, Liam answered in a voice that seemed perfectly normal. "Yo."

"'Yo'? Are you kidding me? What the hell are you doing? Why are you avoiding her?" I shouted.

"If she's afraid of losing the closeness we have, I'll destroy it and rebuild it all over again with a different context."

"What?" I blinked. "That's not how it works! That doesn't sound as cool as you think it does, Li."

"Okay, fine," Liam said with a sigh. "I'm waiting for her to come to me. I don't want to overwhelm her."

"But, Li, she's leaving soon. Like, three days soon."

There was silence on the phone. "I know," he said quietly. "But I know her. I have to wait."

I could hear the sadness in his voice, but he was probably right.

"Try and make sure she's okay," Liam added, and I brought my hand up to my temple.

"What do you think I'm doing?"

"ARE YOU OKAY?" I asked for the hundredth time, genuinely worried as I stopped at Adalia's locker the next day. It was just before lunch, so we had a little extra time. "Are you sleeping?"

"I'm fine," she mumbled unconvincingly, digging through her books. Dark circles draped under her eyes, and her face looked pale. "I've just been thinking about a lot of stuff. Plus, I'm leaving soon, and I still haven't—"

Her head shot up as Liam walked right past us and headed to his locker. The sadness that began to coat her eyes disappeared as another girl came strutting toward Liam.

Both of us were now fully concentrating on what was happening across the hall.

"Hey, Li," the girl chirped, and my heart clenched at the sound of a stranger saying his nickname. I knew if I was upset, Adalia must have been absolutely furious. Out of the corner of my eye, I saw her hand ball into a fist, and it looked like she was biting her cheek.

He turned around, looking surprised and uncomfortable at the same time. It didn't seem like he really knew her, or if he did, he didn't want to. "Oh, uh, hey."

The girl gave a sultry smile as she came closer to him, too close, making a show out of twirling her hair around her finger. Her skirt peeked up just a little higher in the back as she went on her toes. "I haven't seen you with that blond girl lately."

"Oh yeah," he said, turning toward his locker again. He was only across the hall and down a couple lockers, so it was easy to hear what she was saying. It also didn't hurt that she talked loudly, as if showing off.

She continued, "So? Are you finally free? It was really annoying never being able to talk to you, since *she* was always around."

"Uh . . . no, sorry," was his reply. He closed his locker and turned away, but she suddenly grabbed the sleeve of his jacket and pulled him toward her. His eyebrows rose in surprise as she neared his face with squinted eyes.

"Can I change your mind?"

I glanced next to me to watch Adalia's reaction to the whole event, but she wasn't there. My head flashed up as Adalia bolted across the hallway, nearly pushing the girl away from Liam and taking a defensive position in front of him. Liam looked even more surprised as he let his eyes wander her stance.

"No, you can't," Adalia said.

Then she grabbed Liam's hand and stormed out. The two of them turned the corner, and I took a step to follow them before I felt a hand on my wrist pulling me back.

Kyler's voice surprised me. "Wait. They need to figure this out by themselves."

I didn't question when or how he'd gotten here because for some reason, nothing about him surprised me anymore.

We made it to the corner, but we didn't go farther than that. Liam was leaning against the wall of lockers, and Adalia was standing directly in front of him, arguing her tears away.

"You know I'm leaving soon! How could you not even try to talk to me?" Adalia cried, her eyes watering at how hurt she was. But she wasn't just hurt. She was tired and sleep deprived and weak, and I could tell that she was finally going to let her emotions take over.

He took her wrist in his hand and frowned at her. "I didn't talk to you because I knew you'd feel pressured. And I know you're leaving, but I don't care about that, Ad. I like you. I'm going to like you here and when you're in St. Louis or anywhere else in the world. So stop running away from me."

At this, Adalia opened her mouth to argue, to say a come-back, but it looked like she decided against it. Then her eyes were staring at the ground, and she looked lost. "But what about after?" she whispered. "What if you stop liking me? I can't . . . I can't lose you, Li."

"I've liked you since third grade. That's never going to happen." His voice was unwavering. He knew this was the truth.

When Adalia didn't move, Liam tucked his fingers under her chin and forced her to look up at him. They stared at each other for a long moment. Neither of them said a thing. Then finally Adalia, being shorter than him, lifted herself onto her toes and closed her eyes.

Liam smiled down at her, though she couldn't see. But I'd never forget the pure adoration that lit up his eyes just before he met her halfway and their lips finally touched.

If I'd had fireworks, I would have set them off.

MY TWO BEST FRIENDS FOUND ME in the cafeteria a few minutes later. I was halfway through my food when Liam and

Adalia slid into the seats across from me, sitting notably closer to each other than usual.

"So, Brynn, guess what," Liam said, a smile lighting up half his face.

"Hmm. I give up. What?"

Usually he would have fought me on this, making me guess multiple things before finally telling me the answer, but I knew that this time, he wanted to tell everyone as fast as he possibly could about the news.

He put his arm around Adalia in an extremely exaggerated way before pulling her into his side. "She's my girlfriend now. And this time, I didn't use a bug when I confessed."

I couldn't contain my smile. "About time! It was hard watching you two flirt all the time, but at least now you're finally admitting that you like each other." I exaggerated the *like* part just to watch their cheeks turn red.

Adalia's face turned hot as she covered her eyes with her hands. "Oh shut up, you guys."

And in that moment, I didn't care how cringeworthy the two were going to be because they were going to be happier than ever. And honestly, I lived for it.

"It's gonna suck not having you guys around while I'm in Missouri," Adalia said, her tone now taking on a soft edge. Her gaze fell, and Liam pulled her closer.

"You'll be back before you know it." I tried to sound cheerful, especially since they'd just announced the good news. But it was true. She was leaving on Sunday, and there wasn't much we could do to change that.

"You're right," she said, giving a halfhearted smile. "We just have to make the most of my last days."

CHAPTER FIFTEEN

KYLER AND I HAD AN INTERESTING SYSTEM for meeting up. Since his phone was being tracked, we didn't want to risk texting. If we wanted to meet up, we'd leave notes in the gym locker instead, and even then, Kyler would go home, leave his phone there, and then drive to my house. He parked a couple blocks away just to feel better.

Now he was on my couch, his brows creased as he leaned forward and looked at all the evidence he'd gathered splayed on the table. I held his phone in my hands as I watched a video play through his screen. The quality wasn't great, but it was the best he could do considering the circumstances. As ridiculous as it sounded, he'd gotten one of those spy cameras online, the really small ones. Then he'd found a shirt with a front pocket, cut a tiny hole just big enough for the camera lens, and taped the camera against the fabric.

The video started off with Sterling's voice. "Dean is in the office," he said, his voice sounding almost fuzzy with the camera quality. "So let's just say hi. He just wants to see you."

"All right," Kyler responded, his voice crisper and louder.

The camera showed downtown, where old shops and restaurants lined the narrow streets. They continued walking until Sterling stopped abruptly; the sidewalk turned in to an alley that was piled with something tan, maybe sand or dirt, and scattered construction equipment. To the left was a wall covered in bright graffiti, and I knew Kyler had made a point to linger on the building just a little longer. The signs could be used as landmarks.

The camera panned away from the paint and focused on a door, barely recognizable as one as it blended into the wall surrounding it.

When Sterling knocked against it, you could hear a steel clang. The knocking had a certain pattern, and once he was done, a small slit in the door slid open and eyes peered at them from the other side. The person inside must've recognized Sterling because the door opened. Kyler turned just enough to show the doorman's face before they headed down a set of stairs, only barely visible because of a single lamp on the wall.

Groans and excitement erupted as they arrived on the basement floor, and the lights shone brighter. There was a large bar and multiple tables, all crowded with men, some clad in business suits, others in casual clothes. The tables were piled with cards, chips, and stacks of cash; lights shone against red walls, giving the whole place a ruby hue. Kyler spun around, his steps slow as he tried to get as much as he could without drawing too much attention.

"What?" Sterling asked, his voice edging into a laugh. "Never been to a speakeasy before?"

"No," Kyler said. He copied the lightness of Sterling's voice. "It's impressive."

"I know." Sterling sounded proud as he guided Kyler past the tables and toward another shorter, darker hallway that led to just one door. Outside the door stood a man in a dark suit with a gun sticking out of his pocket, which Kyler captured.

The man nodded his head at Kyler. "Who's he?"

"He's with me," Sterling said coolly. "Dean wanted to see him."

The man's expression didn't change, and, after a pause, he stepped aside.

Sterling opened the door with ease, revealing the man called Dean. He looked similar to Sterling, with longer dark hair and a crueler gaze. Something about him was familiar, though I couldn't pinpoint it. Had I seen him before?

Then I realized something—the football game. A man had pushed Sterling onto the ground outside, and although I hadn't seen his face then, the man in front of the camera seemed to fill in the picture perfectly.

"Welcome, welcome," Dean said, his voice almost mocking. "So you're Kyler."

"Yeah," Kyler said. His tone sounded cool and collected. I wondered how hard he'd been trying to not break composure.

"I've heard about you," Dean said. Then he gestured for Sterling to come closer, and as they talked, Kyler twisted around in feigned awe, the camera panning enough to get a glimpse of the general office. Watching the footage made my stomach feel tight with nerves, and I was so thankful he hadn't gotten caught.

When the two brothers were done talking, Dean looked back at Kyler with a grin. "You like it?" He nodded toward the door. "I saw you looking back. You interested in gambling?"

Then he laughed. "You're a little too young."

Sterling copied his laugh, as if it were the funniest thing in the world, and even I chuckled at the fact that anyone could be considered too young to gamble in an illegal gambling ring.

There was more of the video, but it was mostly talking— things that didn't matter much to me but would probably matter to the police.

"This is a lot," I said. I was impressed. He'd taken pictures of account books, lists of "clients" (or victims), and even had a few recordings of when loan sharks were planning on going after people.

Kyler frowned. "But is it enough?"

"Kyler," I said as I sat down next to him. His attention settled on me. "I think I figured out the connection between Ingrid and Adalia."

Kyler's eyes turned alert. "What?"

With a nod, I continued. "Ingrid's dad went to the police about the issue. He didn't know that it would only make things worse. I think they used him as an example, but instead of killing him, they went after Ingrid."

Kyler blinked. "How do you know that?"

"I checked public police records dated around the time Ingrid died. They'd written him off as a drunk, so there weren't that many details, but some of what he had said was documented."

"Wow," Kyler breathed. "You're impressive, Brynn."

I shook my head. "That was easy. You're doing the hard stuff," I said, and he gave me an affectionate grin.

"Anyway, I talked to Adalia over the phone. Her dad finally opened up some more, and he told her that he'd threatened to go to the police. I guess Ingrid's death wasn't a good enough example, so they were going to use Adalia too." I trailed off at the thought. It was so disturbing and disgusting at the same time. People weren't objects, and that was especially true for my best friend.

I tried not to seethe. "That's the connection," I concluded. "So, with your evidence and Adalia's dad's testimony, I think we have a real case. It's exciting, huh?" I continued. "Everything will finally be over."

Kyler nodded. "I can't wait." Then he took my hand. "Let's get everything sorted out tomorrow and contact the FBI."

"Perfect."

Kyler grinned. "And, Brynn?"

"Yeah?"

"Thanks. Thanks for helping me with everything."

My grip tightened around his, and I copied his smile. "You're the one helping me."

He let out a small laugh. "You're right." Then his eyes lit up in realization, and he turned his head toward his backpack. "Did you do your homework for second period?"

"Homework?" My eyes widened at the memory. "Oh my God, homework. I forgot." I dragged my backpack out from under the couch, where I'd accidentally kicked it since I liked to forget about school when I got home, and pulled out a folder.

"This sucks," I said. Kyler settled next to me on the floor and watched as I pulled out an incomplete worksheet.

"I thought you liked psychology?" He smirked.

"It's not my biggest priority right now," I confessed. I reached into my backpack again before my eye caught on something odd. It was a small circular object stuck on the surface of my bag, and when I pulled it off, the bottom part was sticky. I squinted at it. "What is this?"

Kyler peeked over my shoulder. "What?"

I turned toward him, and together we looked at it. "Maybe it got stuck during my camera workshop," I guessed. "That lab has a bunch of random tech things." That didn't sound quite right, but I didn't know what else it could be.

Kyler's eyes squinted in thought before they widened, and he placed his finger over his lips. I didn't quite understand but went along in silence as he gestured for me to hand the backpack to him. He crushed the object between his fingers, and I blinked.

"Better safe than sorry, right?" he said with a shrug.

I couldn't argue with that logic.

AFTER WE FINISHED THE WORKSHEET, Kyler decided to go home. He said his mom was probably waiting to have dinner, so once he left, I decided it would be a good idea to see what I could find in the kitchen. Just as I was pulling out a cereal box, a knock suddenly came from my door.

Although I'd watched Kyler's car leave from my living room window, I figured it was him and walked toward the door, my bare feet padding over the hardwood floor. I wouldn't have been surprised if he'd left something here, as he'd done that before.

I began to open it. "Kyler—"

A glint of umber eyes met mine, and I tried to slam the door shut. Sterling was stronger, though, and pried the door open as I scurried backward.

The only weapon I had was my pepper spray, but that was on my keychain in my room.

His hand gripped my shirt so that I couldn't move, and I felt the hard force of his knuckles collide with my temple. I lost my footing, tumbling onto the floor when he abruptly let go of my shirt. My vision was starting to blur, haze edging my view. This wasn't good. My head felt heavy as I tried to bring it up, but Sterling was on top of me now, pressing a drenched cloth against my nose. Noises of protest came from my mouth as I tried to bring weak hands up to his wrist and push him away. He let out a noise of frustration. "I thought the punch would've been enough. Good thing I brought this in case."

His eyes rested on me. "I hate using it, though. Chloroform takes about five minutes to kick in." He let out what almost sounded like a sigh. "Not that it makes a difference to you."

My eyes darted frantically around the room. He was right; my head was throbbing hard. Yeah, his punch hadn't knocked me out, but it almost had.

What should I do? I couldn't even think straight with so much happening. I only had a few minutes to do something, but my arms were hardly responding as they fell to the floor beside me.

No. I urged myself to do something. I didn't want to die. I didn't know what Sterling would do once I lost consciousness, and that thought alone propelled the fighting instinct in me.

It had been a couple minutes now, and Sterling was starting to look bored as he pushed the cloth farther against my face. He was no longer looking at me but instead at the TV that I hadn't turned off.

I was lying behind the couch and realized the side table was close enough for me to grab. A lamp was placed near the edge, and if I could just will myself to lift my arms . . . maybe I could save myself.

I peeked at Sterling, made another noise, but he didn't seem interested. My arm felt as if it were fifty pounds when I raised it up, slowly, slowly, tracing my fingers against the table legs. My hand inched toward the lamp, and I felt the base in my palm just as Sterling realized what I was doing.

It was too late. I screamed at my limbs to work one final time as I tipped it over with all the strength I could muster. It shattered over his head. Shards flew around the floor, and trickles of blood began to leak down behind his bangs.

It wasn't enough. He was still awake, and my consciousness was fading fast. My body felt limp now, and the last thing I saw before darkness was Sterling's angry scowl.

MY EYELIDS OPENED SLOWLY, revealing a blurred scene of a big, mostly empty room. The walls were tall with small, barred windows near the top; towering black double doors faced me. Metal handcuffs bound my wrists together, and I tugged them apart, just barely, to see how tight they were. I'd never been in handcuffs before, and I wasn't happy that my first time using them was due to kidnapping. My stomach muscles clenched as I leaned forward as far as I could and gained a clear view of the zip ties lacing my ankles together. They were tight enough to dig into my skin, but luckily they didn't hurt too much.

There was an echoed throbbing in my head as I came to my senses. A small *tap, tap, tap* was audible as water leaked somewhere in the room, but it wasn't cold or humid inside. I moved my head from left to right, trying to see if I could recognize anyone; there didn't seem to be anyone in here. Just an empty chair to my right and a table with a laptop on it.

I was about to try to inch my way toward an exit when a hollow voice shook the walls of the room. Dean emerged from the doors, and I had to stare. I'd seen him in the video before, but there was something unsettling about seeing him in person, especially when I was tied to a chair.

"So, she's finally awake," he said, clasping his hands together. Then he called out, "Sterling."

Sterling emerged from behind my chair and arrived quickly by his side. I saw a few bandages above his eyebrows on his forehead and felt slightly pleased that it was because of me.

Seeing Sterling didn't make me feel relieved, but I preferred him to his brother.

"What is this?" I asked, trying hard to keep the trembling out of my voice. His brother's eyes seemed dark, cold even, with the way they pierced through mine. It was more than unnerving, and I turned away. "What's going on, Sterling?"

His throaty voice differed from the polite smiles he'd given every day. "We know what you and Kyler are up to."

His answer took me by surprise, but I should have known. What other reason would they have? My eyes narrowed into slits, and the taller man laughed. "Brynn, right?"

I didn't answer.

"Yeah," Sterling said for me.

"I'm Dean. Dean Reyes." He glanced around the room before leering at me. "Sorry about this. I'm usually better at first impressions, but you know how it is."

Was this guy crazy? My chest clenched. I knew how dangerous it was getting involved in pursuing criminals, but the thought of Sterling being the villain had made it less intimidating. Now I was face to face with someone so much worse, and I realized just how perilous my situation was. This man could kill me. He would kill me without a second thought.

I had to get out of there.

My eyes darted frantically around the room, looking for anything that could possibly help me escape. They'd left me in the room alone before. Maybe they'd do it again, and I could hop out of here with my chair.

The thought of that scenario was ridiculous.

Then a strong hand gripped my chin and jolted my face in the direction of dark, crazed eyes. Dean was sitting in the chair next to me; he'd flipped it around, and his face was close to mine. His deep voice sounded cruel. "Look at me when I'm talking to you."

I had to swallow to keep from crying.

Finally, with all the courage I could muster, I asked in a shaky voice, "What do you want?"

Dean's smile spread. "Now she's asking the real questions." He didn't even look at Sterling as he asked him, "When is he getting here?"

Sterling's voice tried to sound confident, but I could tell he was weak in the presence of his older brother. "Any second."

Dean hummed in satisfaction. As if on cue, footsteps echoed from what I could only guess was a hallway just outside the room. Then both doors slammed open with a force so strong they hit the walls. The chair shook as Kyler rushed in frantically. When his eyes caught mine, he seemed relieved. That relief turned into a glare as sharp as daggers when he noticed the other two.

"What is this?" Kyler gritted.

"Shouldn't we be asking you that question?" Dean said. Every word he spoke was condescending; it was like he thought he was better than everyone.

Dean nodded toward the laptop. "Sterling."

Sterling approached the laptop without a word. Kyler seemed to catch his eye, and for a moment, Sterling smirked. Then he turned to the laptop and tapped a button.

Silence was replaced with the echo of two voices. Mine, then Kyler's. It was a recording of the conversation we'd had at my house just a little while ago. Well, I had to guess it was a while. I didn't know how long I'd been passed out for.

So they knew. They knew we had enough on them to get them locked up for good.

Dean raised an eyebrow. "So? What do you have to say for yourself, Kyler? I thought you were a good member of our team. Loyal, even." He looked down dramatically and sighed. "How unfortunate."

Kyler didn't respond right away. It was like he couldn't. We'd been caught red-handed, and now my life was in danger. But how? How had they gotten the recording?

My blood went cold.

That thing on my backpack. It must have been a bug.

"So now that we're at this point," Dean continued in a drawl, "you have two options. We either kill Brynn now . . ." He paused as he pulled a gun from his pocket. My heart hammered in my chest as he brought it closer to me, closer to my face, and I willed myself to keep my breath steady. A cold laugh rang from his lips as he let the gun loll at his side. "Or you give us every- thing you've collected. Everything. All the evidence: pictures, videos, whatever. If you do that, I'll think about letting your girlfriend live."

"Fine," Kyler bit off.

"Good. Oh, and you have an hour and a half," Dean said, standing up from his chair. He held his hand out lazily.
"Give me your phone."

Kyler frowned. "Why?"

"Give it to me or I shoot Brynn," he said, his free hand twirl- ing the gun.

I knew Kyler was holding himself back as he slapped the phone into Dean's hand, his eyes fierce when they landed on the black-haired man. Dean looked bored as he held the phone up and unlocked it with Kyler's face. Then he was typing rapidly with relaxed brows, and a minute later he handed the phone back to Kyler. "We're tracking you now. You go near cops? We'll know. You call the cops? We'll know. If you run into problems, call me. Otherwise, be here at eight p.m."

Kyler's knuckles turned white as he gripped his phone, but when he caught my eye, his expression softened. "I'll be back, Brynn. I promise."

I gave him the best nod I could before Kyler's brow furrowed and he left. I knew I could trust him, but . . . that wasn't the problem.

Even if he gave them our evidence, they'd still kill both of us. There was no way for them to guarantee we hadn't made copies. There was just no way to make sure we kept our mouths shut unless we couldn't use them anymore.

My hands began shaking in the handcuffs. I didn't know what Kyler was going to do. I didn't know what I would do in his position. All I knew was that I didn't want to die.

I had to admit that I was scared. I was more scared for my life than I'd ever been, and when Dean glanced at me, his sharp eyes full of amusement, I shivered.

"It's cute how much he likes you." Dean grinned, a malicious grin, before standing up from his chair. "I'll be back in an hour. Sterling, stay with her. Make sure she doesn't go anywhere." He looked back at me before he exited, trying to hold in a laugh.

When his footsteps were finally out of hearing range, I had to resist sighing. His presence put me on edge, and though I hated Sterling, he didn't seem as capable.

He stood beside the laptop, cracking his knuckles as he tried to find something to do. A few minutes passed in silence before I finally spoke up.

"You know this is crazy, right?" I said. Maybe if I could convince Sterling to let me go, I could figure something out. The chances were small, though. He seemed weird around his brother, but I knew he was smart—I went to school with him.

Sterling looked my way. "It's not up to me," he said. "Kyler shouldn't have been collecting evidence. And you," he spat, "shouldn't have been encouraging him. Things would have been fine if he just did what we were supposed to do."

I blinked. "You can't really think that. You're in a gang, Sterling. People are dying because of you guys. You really think Kyler would be okay with that?"

He shook his head, a small smile lingering on his lips. "It doesn't matter anymore, does it?"

I bit the inside of my cheek. Kyler had been right about how Sterling was acting different, overconfident. "Sterling," I said.

His head turned back in my direction. "What?"

"How did you guys get the recording of us?"

"You mean your conversation?" He scoffed. "I thought you would've pieced that together. Kyler crushed it, after all."

"I know. I know it was a bug, but why was it on my backpack? How did you even know I still saw him outside of school?" We'd been going the extra mile to just seem like awkward friends after a breakup. There was no way Kyler would've told Sterling that it was just an act.

Sterling's eyes darkened as he looked down. "You know something, Brynn? Kyler thinks he's amazing. Everyone does for some reason—it makes me sick. Going to school and seeing all those people worship him when he's not even doing anything. Me? I have to work for that attention. I had to put on an act to get people to see me the same way. Even when it comes to football; I'm always there on time, early even, and he barely shows up! But guess who everyone loves?" He gave a harsh laugh. "Kyler. But guess what? I was the one who figured out you two still hung out with each other, even if you thought you were being sly. I mean, you could've tried harder to hide it. I saw you two sneaking around at my party, and a couple of guys said something about a girl waiting for Kyler after a football game." When he looked up, his grin was almost crazed. "Who else could it have been but you?"

"So why didn't you bug him?"

"I knew he would expect that. But not you. I figured out what you two were up to, and it was my idea to kidnap you. You're his weakness, which is laughable to say the least, but I knew he'd hand over everything if it meant saving you." He seemed satisfied as he leaned against the table. "It's funny, really. Everyone looks up to Kyler. They think he's so great at everything he does, but I'm the one who won here. I'm the one who beat him. It's not Kyler who's smart or dangerous—it's me."

I almost couldn't believe my ears. Sterling's speech made me speechless; I couldn't decide if I wanted to laugh or cry at how ego driven his actions were. I'd thought that maybe his brother's influence made him pitiful, but I was wrong. He was pathetic all on his own.

My stomach curdled at the idea that he could be one of the last people I saw. I didn't want that to happen. I couldn't let that happen, but I had no control over my life right now.

If there was nothing I could do, I just had to trust that Kyler would find a way to get us out of this mess.

My fingers picked at my nails anxiously. It was the only thing that kept me from falling apart.

"You don't have anything to say to that?" Sterling said, his dark eyes searching my face. "No more questions? You might as well get them all out before you die."

So he was planning on killing me. Even if it wasn't him, it would be Dean. Tears welled up in my eyes, and my heart beat loudly in my ears as I tried to push away the thought.

I really didn't want to die.

I didn't want to engage in conversation with Sterling, either, but it was the only thing I could think of to distract myself.

"Who kidnapped Adalia?" I asked.

"It was Dean," Sterling said.

"It wasn't you?"

"You thought it was?" he replied, a grin almost slipping onto his face. The idea must have been amusing to someone like him. "I set it up. And it was easy, too, considering Adalia gave me her work schedule. Besides, I get things done. You would know. You've seen my work up close and personal, haven't you?"

My blood turned cold when I realized what he was implying. "You mean . . ." I tried to steady my breathing, to not let out a sob. "You were the one who . . . with Ingrid?"

Sterling cackled—it was a cruel sound that cut my ears. "Yeah," he said. "I was the one who pushed Ingrid down the stairs."

CHAPTER SIXTEEN

"TEN MINUTES TILL DOOMSDAY," Dean said from his place on the chair next to me. He sounded excited, like he was anticipating a show. He tucked the side of his gun beneath my chin and raised my face to meet his. "I hope your boyfriend isn't a no-show."

I tried to show as much hatred as I could on my face, but it only made him laugh.

It didn't matter if Kyler was on time. Even if he showed up with the evidence, we'd be goners. Had he had enough time to come up with a plan? With only ten minutes left, I had to believe he had figured something out.

Sterling shifted his weight as he continued to look at the door. He must have been anticipating this moment.

I had to believe in Kyler. There was nothing else I could do.

After another minute or two passed, Dean yawned, and his eyes drifted away from the closed door. "So, Brynn," he started, and I tried not to flinch. I knew I was shaking all over. Blood pounded loudly in my ears, but I tried to ignore it.

I couldn't.

"Did you know Ingrid or something?"

The way he said her name so flippantly made me snap. How could he? How could he talk about her like that after they'd killed her?

Pure disgust showed on my face, and Dean's smile turned into a leer. "Oh, did I hit a nerve?"

He didn't deserve a response from me. I knew everything he said, everything he did, was because he wanted a reaction. I'd never been good at hiding my emotions, but he wouldn't get a word out of me.

"What's the time," Dean called.

Sterling answered, "Seven fifty-nine."

I stiffened at how close we were to the arranged time. Kyler had to come. He wouldn't just leave me here to die.
He couldn't.

What if he did?

"He's really living on the edge, huh?" Dean mused.

Just as he began to say something else, the doors burst open harder than before. Dean jolted upright, and as soon as he processed the situation, he was scrambling up from his chair and making his way behind me.

My eyes watched in astonishment as an entire unit of men and women dressed in bulletproof vests and helmets stalked in, all holding up guns pointed right at Dean. They formed a semi-circle so that people were to the left and right of me, only five or six feet away.

But Dean was holding a gun too. And it was pointed right at my temple. "Take one step closer and I'll shoot."

Every hair on my body stood up. I couldn't breathe. My fear was so intense that my vision started to blur as I scanned the crowd for someone I knew. Kyler? Maybe even Baylor?

"Dean, let's talk," one of the helmeted men said. "There are easier ways to do this."

"For you, maybe," Dean said from behind me. I couldn't tell what expression he was making, but I wasn't too keen on finding out. I noticed Sterling out of the corner of my eye, but he stood still, almost paralyzed. "Not for me."

The sounds of sirens outside the warehouse made it hard to hear, and the flashing lights that shone rhythmically through the small rectangular windows were disorienting. I tried to concentrate on that instead of what was going on in front of me.

"I'm surprised, though. I put someone on Kyler, and nothing seemed suspicious. How did you get here?"

"I'll tell you if you put the gun down," he replied.

"I'm not that curious," he said. The gun that had been pressed against my temple was now an inch away. He must have loosened it without realizing as he talked. "Are you curious, Brynn?" When I didn't respond, his disgusting laugh reverberated around the room. "I guess she's not either."

I didn't know what to do or how this would play out. I just wanted to make it out alive.

"Don't do anything you'll regret," the man said.

Dean gave a wicked cackle. "This isn't something I'd regret."

Then I heard a clank and a shout come from the left side of the room. Dean must have heard it, too, because he frantically turned that way, his gun now pointed outward. Less than a second later, Dean was gasping, or maybe choking, and a sudden thud came from behind me. I took the quick moment to flash my head around; Dean was against the floor, and a woman in the same uniform as the ones in front of me wrestled with him to snap the gun out of his hands.

She must have snuck up and tackled him from the right while he was distracted by the same sound I was.

The gun looked almost free from his hand before he suddenly grasped it and pulled the trigger in my direction.

A sharp pain tore through the outer edge of my torso, and the chair fell over. My binds were still strapped in as I fell with it, and I tried to keep from screaming at the sensation of a bullet scraping against my skin. My chest rose and fell in jolts.

I couldn't believe it. Even after I'd been saved, I'd still been shot. I still could die.

"Brynn!" My name sounded so frantic coming from Kyler's lips. Two familiar faces shoved through the task force; Baylor pulled the chair up, and Kyler held my face in his hands, blue eyes darting across every inch he could see.

"We need pliers!" Baylor called. The ones who weren't holding Dean down and cuffing him rushed to my side; one cut the zip tie that bound my ankles together while someone from behind worked on the handcuffs. I could feel a tiny rustling sensation and wondered if they were using a bobby pin. It didn't matter much to me now as my vision was blurring in pain. I tried to stay focused on Kyler.

"Hey," Kyler said, his hand on my cheek. He drew my attention away from the handcuffs and the pain. His voice sounded loud in my ears compared to the sirens. "Hang in there, okay? We'll get you to a hospital right now."

I was so scared I couldn't answer. My chest trembled as I

finally came undone from the chair, and Baylor swooped me up in his arms.

THE HARSH SCENT OF DISINFECTANT stung my nose. My eyelids fluttered open, squinting at the white that shone from bright lights above. A pounding throb beat against the inside of my head, harder than a hammer, and my eyelids were heavy, trying to close again after I'd just opened them.

"Kyler?" I asked, trying to adjust my eyes to see him clearly. Hospitals were always too bright and uncomfortable for my taste. But at least I was alive.

Kyler sat in the chair positioned right next to my bed, and as I looked closer, I noticed the circles that draped his eyes as he glanced away, his face pale, distraught. His bright eyes weren't meeting mine.

"Kyler," I repeated, this time softer.

Kyler took a peek back at me. "Are you feeling okay?"

"I've been better," I admitted. My wrists and ankles were sore from being bound for so long, and my side . . . well, I didn't want to move. I figured from the IV attached to my arm that I was on pain meds, so I couldn't imagine how I'd feel once they wore off.

He was silent. And when he spoke, his words were hardly a whisper. "I'm so sorry this happened," he breathed as he reached out and placed my hand in his. "I was supposed to protect you."

"What are you talking about? You did."

He didn't say a word as he traced patterns on the skin of my hand. Maybe he didn't believe me.

He touched the sides of my fingers and caressed them as if they were fragile. As if he could break them. I focused on the soft sensations against my skin instead of the pulsating ache from my side.

He intertwined our fingers and brought the back of my hand up to his lips. They grazed against the red of my wrists.

I let go and ran my fingers through his messy brown hair, thinking back to the first time I'd done it. I wanted to touch him forever. I wanted to be with him forever, away from all the bad things we'd gone through.

When he still hadn't said anything, I decided he needed more convincing. "Kyler," I said as gently as I could, "I mean it. You saved my life."

"I didn't know what to do," his hoarse voice said finally. "I . . . I knew I couldn't just do what they told me to. I've never been more stressed out in my life."

"What did you do?" I asked.

"I went home and called Baylor," he said. My eyes widened for a second before thanking the universe for his logic.

"But how? They were tracking your phone."

"They were already tracking it before," he said as he scanned my face. "I think Dean just added extra security when he took it from me. I had a burner phone that I got when I first joined the group. I called him from that."

"I'm so glad he answered," I breathed. "How did you find his number?"

"I had it from our freshmen year group chat. He seemed more prepared than I expected, and he told me to stay home and pretend I was just looking for the evidence while he went and got the authorities prepared. I sent him everything we'd found from my laptop, so . . ." He gave me a weak smile. "I guess it was enough for a case."

"I'm sure my kidnapping probably helped," I joked, but he didn't laugh.

"Are you sure you're okay?" he asked again, his hand clenching mine. "You can barely sleep as it is with your nightmares. This . . ." He frowned. "I'm sorry. I should've been more careful."

"Kyler." When he looked up, I placed his face in my hand and kissed him. He still looked surprised when I pulled back and smiled. I was shaken up too. So shaken up that I hoped my hands didn't tremble when I touched him, but seeing Kyler in this state made me forget about how scared I'd been. It felt like a distant dream, and all that was real was the boy in front of me.

"Stop it. What's done is done. They got arrested, right?"

Kyler blinked before nodding. "Yeah. They got Dean and Sterling. They also got most of the gang members, but they have the full list of names, so whoever ran will be found soon."

"That's great," I said. "That's so great."

"And," he added, his face looking more relieved as he took in my expression, "Baylor told me the cops who were working with them were caught and jailed too. So, you know, they're a little more reliable now."

It didn't feel real. The desperation, the boulder that had weighed on my shoulders, all the pressure I'd been dealing with since the beginning of school instantly melted away. I didn't even notice when a tear of relief began trickling down my cheek. Kyler looked alarmed. "Brynn?"

"I'm so happy," I sniffled. My hands came up to my eyes as I wiped more tears away. "I . . . I can't believe everything's over now."

Kyler's look of concern turned into an easy smile. "Yeah," he said, crinkles now by his eyes. "Everything's over now. You did great."

For some reason, his words of praise were enough to send me over the edge, and now I was bawling into his chest like a child.

I felt his warm hand pat my head. "You were amazing, Brynn."

Once I was out of tears and no longer clinging on to Kyler's shirt, a knock came from the door. "Brynn?"

"Come in," I replied. Blond hair peeked in from the door, and Baylor gave a relieved smile. Kyler must have read the room because he stood up.

"I'm gonna get some water," he said. Baylor caught his eye just before he slipped through the door, and I wondered what the relationship between them was like now. Baylor paced forward and took a seat on the chair next to me.

"How do you feel?" he asked, concern etched into his face. At the sight of my older brother's worry, I suddenly felt guilty. I knew I should have told him what I was up to, especially since things had reached this point, and my excuses for not saying anything were selfish.

"I'm feeling fine," I said. My voice came out softer as I continued, "I'm sorry, Baylor."

"Yeah? Good." He sat back in the seat and crossed his arms. Then he gave an exasperated sigh. "I've known something was up for a while, you know."

"I know," I mumbled. And I did, considering how clingy he'd become the past few weeks. I didn't know how much he knew, of course, but I figured Baylor's pride would probably tell me.

"You didn't really think I wouldn't know about Adalia, right?" He shook his head. "This isn't a big city. Matt told me about a kidnapping, and it was easy to find out the victim was Adalia when I looked at the local news and social media. It made sense, too, especially since I called you that night and you blew me off."

His light eyes bored into mine, and I looked away sheepishly. "But I don't care about that," he said, his voice gentle now. "You guys are safe. Everything's over now, and that's what I care about."

"Baylor . . ." I couldn't contain the affection that swelled up in my chest as I leaned over and hugged him. He wrapped his arms firmly around me and gave a pat as I buried my face in his shoulder. "I'm sorry," I said again.

"It's okay."

When I pulled back, he was smiling.

"I know you care about my safety. And I knew you'd stop me from getting involved, so I couldn't say anything," I explained. "I really wanted to tell you. I just . . . I was too focused on it. I wanted to find out what happened no matter what."

"Well, you did," Baylor said. He didn't sound mad. "You did good, B."

I gave a wide grin. "You think so?"

"Yeah." Baylor chuckled. "Aside from getting kidnapped, you did pretty well."

"Speaking of," I started, "what happened? Kyler said he called you."

"Your boyfriend's smarter than he looks," Baylor said, and I knew Kyler would've been offended. "To be honest, I'd been doing some of my own digging too. When you told me about Ingrid and that you were hanging out with Sterling . . . I just thought it was weird timing. So I looked more into Dean's whereabouts to see what city he'd moved to, what his old friends were up to, that kind of thing. It was just personal curiosity that got me started, so when Kyler called, it wasn't hard to convince me."

I blinked. "Wow." I shook my head. "But what else did you find? Did you talk to the FBI?"

"I talked to them—it all went really fast. I explained the situation over the phone while they looked over the evidence, and the fact that you were a hostage made everything move quickly," he said. "And about what I found . . . all his old friends had the same job here, and no one seemed to know where he was. I looked at Sterling on social media, too, and noticed he'd started posting a lot more name brands. Expensive things. I was worried that he was still hanging around you, so I guess I couldn't help but check in so often. Sorry if it got annoying."

I shook my head quickly. "You're not annoying. Thank you so much for caring about me, Baylor. I'm sorry I didn't say anything. Maybe things would've worked out differently." I held back a wince at the sting in my side, and Baylor put his hand on my head.

"Things work out the way they're supposed to. Everyone got caught, you're alive and safe now, and the city can stop worrying about Dean's group." He grinned. "I'd say you did pretty good."

I let out a laugh. "Pretty good?"

"Really good."

I leaned in for another hug and smiled into his chest as he said one more thing.

"Just don't do it again."

EPILOGUE

"YOU KNOW WHAT I HEARD?" Liam asked as he threw a fry into his mouth. We sat at our round table in the school cafeteria, and everything seemed like it was normal again.

Adalia sat close to his side, her green eyes glistening as they always did when Liam talked. She hadn't had to stay in St. Louis very long, which all three of us were pretty happy about. The town was as safe as it had always been now, and I couldn't deny that I was feeling a little proud at having helped it get back on track.

Kyler sat next to me, stealing fries off my tray like he always did whenever I had to eat lunch from the cafeteria. I'd been in a hurry this morning, and there were no leftovers from dinner last night, despite how much food my mom had made for us.

I'd been so glad to have my parents back. They'd taken the first plane to Colorado once they found out about my kidnapping. And, well, let's just say the ride back from the hospital was very emotional.

They vowed to never go on a business trip for longer than a week while I was still in school, and personally, I liked that idea. Now my mom was trying to make it up by cooking fancy dinners almost every night. I liked that idea too.

"What did you hear?" I asked Liam. His full lips beamed as he looked at Kyler.

"Your boyfriend over here is back to full power," Liam said. Adalia and I threw each other confused looks.

"Meaning . . ." Adalia started.

"Meaning," Liam elaborated, "he's the number one most wanted guy at Westwood now that Sterling's gone and there's no competition." He paused. "Well, aside from me."

I rolled my eyes at his joke. It was true that Sterling was gone, and although the arrest had happened a month ago, the school was still brimming with gossip over the whole thing. It truly was scandalous, especially for a town like this, but I didn't love the fact that my boyfriend was now a target of affection for hundreds of teenage girls. Then again, was he even my boyfriend? He'd never actually asked me out, and we never brought it up.

I must have been making a weird face because Kyler tilted his head toward me in that questioning way.

The school cafeteria was probably not the best place to ask, especially not in front of my two best friends, who would tease me endlessly for it, so I shook my head.

Once my final period was over, Kyler met me at my classroom door. He kept his keys on a lanyard that he liked to swing around, and when he saw me, he stopped. "Ready to go?"

We'd gotten into the routine of Kyler driving me to and from school, which was his idea, and I'd never protested it. I wasn't the biggest fan of driving anyway, plus it meant we got to spend a few more minutes together alone.

"Yeah," I said. He intertwined our fingers thoughtlessly as we walked out to the parking lot. I always liked it when he held my hand, and I didn't think he realized how much he did it. It was one of the first things I'd noticed about him, and it was also one of the things I hoped would never change.

When we were finally on the road, he turned the music down. "By the way," he said, "were you feeling okay during lunch? Did Liam's comments bother you?"

I couldn't help but feel touched. He was always paying attention to the smallest things about me. "It's not that, but . . ." I looked away and out the window. I almost didn't want to ask, but I dug up the courage and spat it out. "Are we dating?"

I felt the car swerve for half a second before Kyler pulled it back between the lines. With widened eyes, I turned toward him, and he coughed.

"Was it that surprising?" I asked, just as shocked.

"I . . ." He thought about his words and then burst out laughing. I blinked at him.

I was in the car with a crazy person.

"Brynn," he said, his eyes still crinkled, "I'm sorry. I . . . I didn't realize I never asked you out."

"What, so you just forgot?" I asked, crossing my arms. It wasn't a big deal, but I was a little embarrassed.

"Yeah," he said. He turned to look at me when he got the chance and smiled. "Genuinely. There was a lot going on when we first started talking, you know? Plus, everyone already thought we were dating, and I guess I forgot we never actually were."

We were getting close to my house when he pulled over and

turned toward me. The pout on my lips must have made him laugh again, and I sighed.

"You're so annoying," I mumbled.

"Aw, Brynn," Kyler said teasingly. "C'mon."

When I refused to look his way, he leaned even closer. "You know I've always thought of you as my girlfriend. I mean, you've met my mom. You've even had dinner with us. Plus, I've met your entire family. Everyone at school knows we're together. I drive you to school every day. I kiss you every chance I get. I—"

My hand found its way over his lips, and now it wasn't stubbornness that kept me from looking at him. It was the red on my cheeks. He was so good at making me feel embarrassed when he listed things off like that, and he knew it.

I felt his lips kiss the inside of my palm as he wrapped his fingers around my wrist and gently pried them away. "Brynn," he said. "Look at me."

I peeked out of the corner of my eye and cursed him for the millionth time for being so attractive. Whenever I saw his face, I didn't want to look away. His blue eyes caught mine, and I finally gave in. "I'm looking," I murmured.

He chuckled. "You're so cute."

When I began to look away again, he tugged me toward him and made me watch as he lifted my knuckles to his lips. Then he grinned. "Brynn," he said, "will you be my girlfriend?"

I didn't realize how much I'd wanted to hear those words. When he said them, I felt my lips waver into a smile, and the glint in his eye proved he knew exactly what I was thinking.

"Maybe," I said playfully. "If you buy me dinner first."

"Are you free tonight? Sushi?" he asked.

"Perfect."

It was just like the first time he'd asked me out. I'd felt terrified and thrilled at the same time. I still felt that way, only now it was more thrilled. Thrilled that I was getting a free meal, of course, but more thrilled that I was with Kyler.

We'd come so far that it was almost unbelievable.

And it'd all started with a locker.

ACKNOWLEDGMENTS

First and foremost, I have to genuinely thank everyone who read *The Locker Exchange* on Wattpad. Seeing the comments and reads, any type of support really, was what pushed me to keep writing chapters even when I struggled with it. Your reactions to watching the whole story play out were such a joy for me to see; finding out which characters you liked and what made you squeal or cry made the entire experience incredible, and I can't thank you guys enough for enjoying the story.

The love I hold for all of you is more than I can describe.

So this book is for you.

To Deanna, Rebecca, and Fiona, my editors, for guiding me along this process and never losing faith. You helped me take one step at a time and, slowly but surely, shape this book into what I'm proud it's become.

And finally, my family. Thank you to my dad especially, for believing in me more than I sometimes believed in myself. I'm truly grateful to have a family that supports me in everything I do, and this book is just one result of the unconditional love I've been lucky enough to receive from you.

Thank you to everyone.

All my love,

Ann

ABOUT THE AUTHOR

ANN RAE has been expressing herself through stories ever since she could talk. Since then, her film degree has given her a broader view of narrative, helping her to create and immerse herself in stories of any form. Half Taiwanese, Ann spends a lot of time both in the US and Asia and often draws inspiration from her personal experiences. She started posting her stories online when she was thirteen years old, and her debut novel, *The Locker Exchange,* has amassed over twenty-six million reads and forty-six thousand followers on Wattpad. Ann currently resides in Colorado.

Turn the page for a preview of

Available wherever books are sold.

TIP ONE:
DON'T OVERREACT; UPGRADE

✳

People might consider me ever so slightly *overdramatic*.

But I pride myself on the fact that I have the perfect amount of drama *and* paranoia for the average teenager. For example, I may have performed multiple soliloquies in front of my mirror this morning, practicing what I would say to my best friends after not seeing them for the entire summer because my family and I were in the Philippines. I also may have pictured the absolute worst-case scenario that could happen at school, which is basically a zombie apocalypse preventing me from *escaping* the school (and also my friends completely ghosting me). All of the above is natural, human behavior. It has *nothing* to do with the potentially catastrophic, life-altering first day of grade twelve.

Stepping into the Keele Street–side entrance of the school, I open the infamous LKJC (a fun acronym for Lara, Kiera, Jasmine, and Carol) group chat to ask my friends if they're around.

Me: *You guys here yet?*
Kiera: *Yeah, at our usual spot*

We've claimed a particular section of the hallway near the art department on the third floor as our spot. With large windows that overlook the first-floor atrium, it's where we've been doing our morning meetups since tenth grade.

> **Jasmine**: *Not Carol, though, she's probably going to get detention on the first day for being late LOL*
> **Me**: *For real ha-ha*
> **Carol**: *Wowwww I'm literally 2 minutes away!*
> **Kiera**: *Sureee . . .*
> **Carol**: *It's true! Watch, I'll be there in less than 5*
> **Jasmine**: *Okayyy . . .*

I manage to huff my way up three flights of yellow-painted stairs to the third-floor landing. Needing one last moment to compose myself (and my heavy breathing) before pushing the doors open, I sweep some stray hairs away from my glasses and pull out my cell phone to take one last look at my reflection. The straightener did its job because my long, black hair is still not frizzy. The T-shirt tucked into baggy jeans looks cute enough, and my white shoes are . . . they're not white anymore, but it's *fine*.

One last breath. *Inhale. Exhale.*

Pushing the heavy metal doors open, I stride confidently into the packed hallway. By "confidently," I mean that I manage to walk without falling, tripping, or doing anything remotely embarrassing. Schedule in hand, I search for my friends, but am greeted instead by half-asleep fellow seniors and frantic, stray puppyesque freshmen heading to their classes twenty minutes early.

Turning left at the next hallway, I finally see two of the three girls. Kiera is gesturing frantically (probably talking about an anime or her own life drama) and Jasmine, leaning her head against the blue lockers, is either uninterested or sleepy.

Jasmine looks the same; her short black hair still in a bob with bangs clipped to the side. With each passing year she looks more like her mom, who has dark eyes that kiss in the corners and rosy cheeks against pale skin. The only difference between them is that everything Mrs. Zhao wears is fresh off of the runway, while Jasmine values simplicity over anything else. Today that means Jasmine's got on a light-gray cardigan with cropped denim capris.

Unlike Jasmine, Kiera's appearance has changed from when I last saw her in June. Her strawberry-blond hair, which used to be down to her waist, is cut to her shoulders, with loose curls framing her face. Nevertheless, I notice her girly style is still in place as she adjusts her lavender sundress.

Their outfits match their personalities almost exactly. Jasmine has been my best friend/neighbor since kindergarten, and even then she was the shy type. Being the true introvert of our friend group, it makes sense that she dresses to blend in. She's also the only one who's mature enough to keep the rest of us in line.

Kiera Jones is exactly as bubbly as she looks. Everything about her is bright, from her dress to her hair to her eyes to the smile that never fades. Speaking of bright, we became friends in kindergarten after she drew a flower on my hand with a neon-pink marker, for the sole reason of matching the drawing on hers. It took a week to wash off, but our friendship has lasted since then. She has a natural charm that can attract just about every type of person, making her friends with almost everyone at school, and is the girl people instantly fall for.

Yet she's never been in a romantic relationship. None of us have, except for Carol. But we like to disregard Carol's one and only ex-boyfriend because that fling only lasted a month and ended with a whole lot of Taylor Swift songs (the angry ones, not the sad ones).

Sometimes I find it weird that my friends never accept any of their suitors. Jasmine has had at least three cute guys ask her out, all of whom she accidentally ghosted because she's oblivious. Kiera simply rejects people on the spot. Carol uses an intensive interrogation process to weed out the candidates. And me? Nobody ever asks me out. I think they're either intimidated by the fact that I'm the perfect package deal or they've witnessed my early morning hallway monologues, in which I argue that real men will never live up to fictional ones. Our shared lack of interest in a partner keeps us on the same page. We're all able to keep the perfect balance between our separate lives, school, extracurriculars, and of course, each other. Best of all, there's no relationship drama to get in the way.

As I rush toward them, a sudden jolt of energy bursts through my body, like I've had one too many caffeinated drinks. I've *really* missed them.

Spending July and August in my parents' hometown in the Philippines has resulted in me now being two shades darker than usual and having mosquito-bitten legs. It was a family reunion with relatives I hardly knew existed, and if you've ever seen a complete Filipino family, you'd probably mistake it for a small village, which is funny because we were *literally* in a small village. Unlike most of our other Fil-Can friends, my parents didn't come from Manila or any of the big cities. Their home is somewhere in the rural part of Batangas, where water only runs during the early morning and late night and *butiki* crawl up the walls. For a girl who's lived in Toronto her whole life, let's just say culture shock smacked me in the face. But the biggest adjustment I had to make was the absolute lack of internet, which meant not communicating with my best friends for almost two whole months.

"Kiera! Jasmine!" I shout, waving my hands.

Their faces light up as they wave back. I am about to do that movie running scene–thing when a foot comes out of nowhere and I trip, landing on the ground and doing away with my attempt to get through the day without embarrassing myself. I maneuver my body so that I'm at least *sitting* on the floor instead of lying down on my stomach. When the culprit's eyes meet mine, the familiar feeling of disgust sets in. That *idiot*.

He holds a handout to help me up. I make the stupid decision to take it. Midway, he releases my wrist, sending me back on my butt. *Wonderful*. Stifled laughs from bystanders are met with my own glares. Annoyed, I get up, scowling at his devilish smile. By devilish, I mean that he reminds me of an actual demon that escaped from hell.

I am by no means a hateful person. I'm never a part of any school drama and honestly, aside from corrupt world leaders and conceited people, I don't hate anyone, except one specific boy I've known since birth; one I would've murdered a long time ago if his mother wasn't best friends with mine—Jameson Bryer. James for short. Or The Idiot. They're interchangeable.

Getting up from the ground, I narrow my eyes at him. "Do you wake up every day asking the underworld for a checklist of things to help make the world a terrible place?" While going to war with each other is usually our thing, I refrain from kicking him where the sun doesn't shine because it's Tuesday morning and frankly, revenge is a second day of school thing.

James runs a hand through his dark-brown hair. "Of course not. Unlike you, I am a descendant from the heavens." He presses his palms together in a prayer gesture then draws an imaginary circle above his head. "I haven't seen you in two months. How much have you missed me?"

My right eye twitches slightly. Because my love for his family is the only thing keeping me from pushing him off the nearest cliff, I say, "You know the distance between here and Jupiter? That, times negative one."

"Sad to see you haven't changed."

While I was away in the Philippines for the summer, he went on a luxury cruise in the Bahamas—and I had the pleasure of not seeing his face until today.

"I can only say the same about you," I retort. "You'd think that two months would give you enough time to plan a more *creative* greeting, but I see you're plagiarizing tactics."

He takes a step forward, closing the distance between us. "Well, sweetheart, I live by the saying an eye for an eye. You tripped me two months ago, so I'd say revenge was awfully overdue."

"That was an accident!"

He raises an eyebrow.

"Accidentally . . . on purpose," I admit. "But you were being infuriating that day and that trail was supermuddy and you know that I *don't* hike and—" I clamp my mouth shut when I notice the amusement on his face. This is what he wants. He wants me to run my mouth until I slip up and he can tease me for it. And since I am not giving him the satisfaction of doing that today, I give him a curt nod before turning around, finishing our conversation.

Walking over to my friends, I hold my head high even though everyone is looking at me. At this point, I don't feel bothered by their stares; it's the common aftermath of my James encounters. My *frustrating* James encounters. Kiera and Jasmine stand beside the lockers, both trying to look supportive, though I can sense the secondhand embarrassment radiating off of them.

"Do you think I'd get caught if I took some eggs from the caf and egged his car?" I ask.

They laugh, lightening the mood. Though I controlled myself

earlier, everyone knows that I never back down from James. Sure, he's the school's beloved star hockey player, but I'll retaliate when provoked. It's the reason why our personal attacks on each other never seem to end. Fighting is our thing. Our feud was established when it was decided that we'd both exist on the same planet. In fact, I should have been prepared for a sneak attack like that trip in the hall. I'd let my guard down and it won't happen again.

"I'm here! I'm here!" Rapid steps approach as Carol runs toward us in her Adidas joggers, bright blue cleats in her arms and her bag half falling off her shoulder.

The best way to describe Carol Gonsalves is chaotic. She's the friend who's either late, underdressed, or says something completely inappropriate out of the blue. She joined our friend group in the fifth grade when her family immigrated from Goa and has been my partner in pranks ever since. I don't think I'd terrorize James as effectively without her. "Ha! Told y'all," she says, pointing a finger at us. "I was here in less than three minutes. What did I miss?"

Jasmine says, "The public humiliation of Lara."

"What do you mean?" Carol mumbles, holding a hair tie between her front teeth as she gathers her long black locks into a bun.

"Let's just say that Lara and James's dynamic has not changed," Kiera says.

I let out a large breath. "Unfortunately, that entails him tripping me on the first day of school."

After Carol finishes wrapping the elastic around her mass of hair, she punches me in the shoulder, expecting an interesting story. "I came too late! Bro, what did you do to him?"

"Nothing." I shrug.

"No, seriously! What did you do? Did you twist his arm? Did you kick him in the—"

"I ignored him."

She stops chuckling immediately and frowns, nostrils flaring. "What happened to you on vacation that you suddenly turned to the *good side*?" Carol grips my shoulders and shakes me back and forth until I feel like I'm about to hurl. "Get yourself together, woman! I did not raise you like this!"

"Dude, *calmes-toi*, I don't want to start my day off with negative vibes," I say, and she pretends to wipe a bead of sweat off her forehead. "Now forget about him. What were you guys up to while I was gone?"

Their eyes widen like criminals that have been spotted, like deer caught in headlights. Jasmine fidgets with her fingers, Kiera bites her lip, and Carol looks ready to bolt even though she *just* got here.

"Is it about Mark?" Mark was a guy from the soccer team, and he obviously liked Carol. They'd been hanging out for a while now, but I wasn't sure if their friendship would become something more. Did something happen over the summer?

No one replies. *They're not telling me something.*

"I'm not telling her," Jasmine squeaks. Kiera shakes her head, too, following Jasmine's lead.

They both look at Carol, knowing that she always does the best at explaining situations. She approaches me and places a hand on my shoulder, frightened eyes becoming round circles. Not that I'm a scary person . . . just a bit *unpredictable*. "Don't freak out on us but . . ."

There's a new commotion behind us, distracting me from the conversation and forcing my head to turn. James yells to his friends as they emerge from the other hallway, walking over and greeting them wildly with complex handshakes and backslaps. Meanwhile, the other students stare at them like they're celebrities. In this high school setting, I suppose they are. All it takes is above average physical genetics mixed with athletic ability to create a popular person, right?

But if being popular is the same as being well known, then I suppose I'm pretty popular as well. Not because I'm athletic but because James and I almost kill each other on the daily, and if they're looking at him, they're also looking at me.

James walks with his crew following closely, drawing the eyes of *everyone*. Usually in the movies, you'd see the mean girl and her squad, but this is a guy version of that. Imagine a rock song from a 2000s coming of age movie playing in the background. Then imagine the confident Regina George stride. Now mix that with four good-looking student athletes but subtract the problematic attitudes, since James's squad consists of fairly nice people who are unfortunate enough to be friends with the idiot.

Among the unlucky, is Mark Medina—James's oldest friend from elementary school and one of mine too. He's cute in the same way that a puppy is, but shy. I always wondered how he ended up being friends with a demon, considering he's a literal angel from the heavens, or as he likes to say, *Lara, for the hundredth time, I'm from Peru.* To be fair, the top of Machu Picchu is pretty close to the sky.

Then there's Daniel Samuels. I can't say much about him because I don't know him all that well. He's the smart one of the group, and besides playing hockey, he's the president of the debate club. He's Black, with long braided cornrows and a charming smile that naturally causes people to gravitate toward him. Less shy than Mark but not as boisterous or obnoxious as James.

Lastly, we have Logan Ford, who is neither shy nor bright. I'm not saying this to be mean, but in grade nine geography class he confidently stated that Brazil was located in Europe. There's that, and the fact that he's a literal representation of the stereotypical blue-eyed, blond-haired player that you see in every other Netflix film. He's always been nice to me, but his reputation for going through girls as if the yearbook was a dating checklist has been enough to keep me away.

They all have updated looks from when we last saw them in June. Daniel's style has evolved, now playing with more color and pattern; Logan sports a summer tan, a striking contrast to his natural fairness; and Mark has a fresh haircut, chopping off his usual shoulder-length locks.

I turn back to my friends, ready to ask about why they're so nervous, when I hear the voice of one of James's squad members.

"Babe!"

Spinning around so fast that my head could fall off if it wasn't attached to my body, my attention focuses on a certain shy boy now running over to my group. *Mark?* Carol grins at me shyly as he wraps an arm around her shoulder. She brushes his dark-brown curls away from his green eyes. Nausea threatens to overwhelm me, but I keep my expression under control. "Looks like we're going to be third wheels!" I chirp to Kiera and Jasmine, who don't return my smile or laugh at my joke like they would normally.

"Darling!" another guy shouts, causing a cringe to form on my face. *Darling? Are we in the 1960s now?*

Daniel races toward us. *Who is he going—*

He wraps his arms around Kiera and kisses her forehead.

Oh my goodness, no.

"Honey!"

Whipping my head around once more (okay, I did get whiplash this time), I see Logan sprinting toward us. Pushing me out of the way, he attacks Jasmine's face with his own, as if she's in a life-threatening condition and needs immediate CPR. And this is why honey belongs in a beehive and not in a school hallway.

What the heck is going on? And where is the nearest trash can so I can vomit?

Carol, fine. We all saw that coming. She and Mark have been close for almost five months. Kiera, kind of weird. She's not really the type to date with her overloaded schedule. But *Jasmine*? Jasmine Zhao is a freaking saint! We all thought she was going to become a nun or something! *Can someone fetch me a glass of water? Actually, can you make it holy water?* Yet here she is, hand-deep in his blond hair, making out with Logan Ford, the blue-eyed mega player of the school. Don't tell me I missed the good-girl, bad-boy story arc while I was gone. Staring at the three couples for a minute, I consider all the ways that I could chase these boys off with a sledgehammer.

Breaking away from the kiss, Jasmine says, "Lara, don't freak out, we can expl—"

"What the hell is *this*?" I shout at the top of my lungs, gesturing at the three members of James's squad who have attached themselves to my best friends like leeches.

I look at Carol and Mark, Kiera and Daniel, Jasmine and Logan, and finally at James, who is, thankfully, as confused as I am about this situation.

"Guys?" he asks his friends, an eyebrow raised.

Mark says, "Sorry, bro, we couldn't reach you for the whole summer. You literally did not reply to our group chat for a month."

"Yeah, Lara, you had no signal so . . ." Kiera adds.

James and I have the exact same expression on our faces. I don't know if I'm going to go ballistic or if I'm going to faint. I turn to Jasmine. "You too? You told me that you wouldn't date until you graduated!"

"I know, I know, but it sort of just,"—she looks lovingly at her boyfriend (gross)—"happened."

"You guys are actually committing to a relationship?" James says, and I narrow my eyes at him. Classic James, moving on from one girl to the next as if they're objects. Seeing my repulsed expression, he sticks his hands up and quickly adds, "I'm just kidding, sweetheart, don't be such a buzzkill."

Oh, I could kick him right now. *Self-control, Lara, self-control.*

"Oh yeah," he adds. "Sorry about my nonexistent replies in the group chat. My phone actually fell into the ocean, and I just got a new one."

"Ocean?" Daniel raises an eyebrow.

"You don't notice a lot of things when you're salsa dancing on the deck with a hot girl." James steps forward and back with his eyes closed—a motion that seems like a dance, but I can't call it that. A smile plays on his lips as he thinks back to the event.

"*Anyway—*" I start, but Kiera jumps in before I can continue.

"Lara, we'll explain everything to you at lunch. Promise." She gives my right shoulder a reassuring squeeze before grabbing Daniel's hand and doing that nasty, romantic eye-contact thing. Lunch. Along with stressing about the line for cafeteria french fries, I'm stressing about *this*. Their boyfriends. My french fries. Boy-fries, as we'd once called them as elementary kids.

The warning bell rings, and the three couples go hand in hand into the sunset—well, to their first period classes.

James and I stand frozen in our places, exchanging glances before continuing to watch our friends' backs get farther away. We usually face very different problems, but today we're united on one common front. Our friendships are screwed. How is it possible to have upgraded to a seventh wheel?

I sit at the back of my first period English class, dumbfounded. In the two months that I was away, my friends just *happened* to bump into three hot guys, changing their relationship status from single to not-so single. I tap my long nails on the hardcover English textbook, trying to absorb the new information without hyperventilating.

Right as my breathing returns to normal, Logan and Daniel walk into the classroom. Noticing the empty seats beside me, Logan sits on my left, sandwiched between me and Daniel. They both have gleeful expressions on their faces, obviously not understanding the trauma they induced earlier. It makes me want to scream. Here I was, thinking that I was incredibly lucky to have a friend group void of relationship drama; that all of us were on the same page. Now, I'm sitting beside two people responsible for this unwanted new chapter, who shrink in their seats as I glower at them.

"Lara, I really like Kiera and I'm so sorry that we never told you until now," Daniel explains. "It just kind of happened during the summer." His dark eyes hold enough sincerity that I have difficulty keeping the angry expression on my face.

"And I really like Jas. Like really, *really*, like her," Logan says, but I'm less convinced. I'm sure he's really, *really* liked a lot of girls, considering he has a new one each week. "I know what you're thinking. And she's different. I'm different with her."

The words *she's different* and *I'm different with her* immediately activate my defensive parent mode because goodness gracious, I've read enough books to know that this foreshadows a lot of relationship bumps.

"Listen," I hiss at Daniel, "if you ever do anything to make Kiera cry, I swear on my life, I will hunt you down and beat you until you can't move."

Daniel begins to nod but pauses. "Okay, I'm not going to hurt her, but you do realize we're talking about *Kiera*, right? The other day I showed her a *car commercial* and she cried because there was a puppy. Can we negotiate this agreement? Perhaps only beat me up if her tears are caused by my *mistakes*?"

How did my overly emotional best friend end up with a guy who interprets threats using logic?

"Or not," he says, caving under my intense stare. "It's fine."

Then it's Logan's turn. "And you, I get that you think that you're a 'nice person' and all, but we all know about that speed dating crap you pull on girls. Jasmine *doesn't* need a player."

"I know," he says, shaking his head and frowning like he'd never consider hurting Jas. "I'm serious about her. I've never felt this way about anyone."

"*Sure.*"

I pull out my phone just as Logan begins to respond. "I promise I've changed. I'm . . . Lara, are you listening?"

"You know, Logan, I've been thinking about capitalism lately, and how much I like money."

"*Okay?*"

"I've also been thinking about intestines and, well, how fitting that you have some." Looking up from my cell phone, I calmly ask, "Logan Ford, do you know how much intestines are worth on the black market?"

"No?"

He might not but my Google search page does. Sliding my phone to the center of his desk, I watch in amusement as his blue eyes widen with fear. I've never seen someone so terrified of numbers. His frozen stature is enough confirmation that the threat has been received, so I reach for my cell phone and shove it back into my pocket.

Finally, our English teacher walks into the room. "Good morning, everyone!" he greets us as he places his coffee mug on the desk. "My name is Mr. Garcia and we'll be spending the first period of the whole semester together. The assigned locker list is on the back wall, and at the end of class I'll be handing out the personal information sheets for you to take home and fill in. How does that sound?"

As usual, the class full of sleep-deprived teenagers does not show any sign of response. Half of them have their phones in their laps, checking their social media as if something has changed within the past minute.

"I'll take that as a yes. Now, on your desks you'll find our short story textbook, which we'll be using for unit one. Please turn to page five and take a moment to read over the first story," he instructs, and the sound of flipping pages takes over the room.

While some students begin the reading, others have her books standing upright, attempting to hide their cell phones. Mr. Garcia sighs, eyeing one of the students in the corner of the room. "Richard, can you please get off the phone."

"I'm not even on it! I'm reading!" he says defensively, pointing to the erect book, which, unfortunately for his case, is upside down.

This is going to be a long day, I think to myself.